Into the BeanStalk

Book One of the Jack: Cyberpunk Series

J. Paul Roe

Get the free short-story prequel to the *JACK:* series at www.jpaulroe.com!

Contents

"History makes no attempt at hiding humankind's knack for mishandling progress, nor our skill at weaponizing the mundane."

– From *Mind Shackles: Post-Collapse Technocracies* by Zathura Aster.

Chapter One

POINTS

August of rank wind blew from the denser parts of the city, driving an obnoxious dervish of yellow sand right into my face. Strands of ice-white hair escaped from under my hoodie and poked me in the eye.

This was gonna be a good day. I could already tell.

Brushing my hair aside with one hand, I tapped a string of code into the warehouse's side door with the other. Lights blinked green, and the thick metal door popped open with a faint clunk. A blast of moldy, stale air rushed out from the dark interior and slapped the other side of my face.

"'Bout time," the guy beside me whispered in a rough voice. "Now stay low and outta my way while I do my thing."

That was Slick, a lifelong member of the Luckies and a dirty, not-too-bright goon. He pushed me aside and slid into the building while I disconnected my palm interfacer from the door controls.

The 'facer was a handheld refurb with a manufacturing date older than my first birthday, but it worked like shiny new. I took care of my stuff and my stuff took care of me.

Guys like Slick weren't really on the same page when it came to maintenance. Teeth missing, hair all patchy, and smelling like roadkill pretty much constantly. Like the rest of the gangers I'd been wrapped up with, he didn't take care of anything except his precious motorcycle.

Slick cared even less about me than he cared about hygiene, so he walked ahead without ever looking back to see if I was following him. I trailed him in, natch, but he wouldn't acknowledge my presence again until he needed another door opened or a security panel cracked.

It was anybody's guess if this heap of a warehouse had much functioning tech left to work with. The old building was three stories tall and nearly as big as Hanska Stadium, but was mostly empty except for row after row of broken industrial cargo racks and some random piles of junk. Just enough to give Slick some cover to creep around the inside wall with me trailing behind – and downwind.

About halfway through the junkheap interior, Slick stopped and lowered himself to a crouch.

"Aww, yeah," he whispered, waving me over with a coal-black cybernetic arm.

I slipped behind him and gripped the knife sheathed at my waist. My SevenArms MMK multi-mission knife was the most advanced piece of hardware I had to my name. Fresher than my wetgear, newer than my interfacer, and really damn sexy as far as knives go.

Nearly as long as my forearm and laser sharp, the "multi-mission" part meant that it had a tech-augmented blade and a cartridge system in the hilt. Want an electrified blade? There's a cartridge for it. Poison blade? There's a cartridge for that. Blade projecting superheated plasma for cutting a car door in half? Yup, that too.

Of course, I didn't *have* any of the cartridges, myself. You don't get the full starter kit when you klep your multi-knife from a passed-out corporate foot soldier in an alley.

But still, that's what I'd brought to this potential gunfight – a knife. Not by choice, but because my bond to the Luckies didn't allow me to carry hot steel on a job.

Slick, on the other hand, was a full-blown Lucky that had earned his ink a long time ago, many times over, and he was well-armed. His cybernetic wetgear wasn't all that impressive, just a pair of consumer-grade arm replacements with a flat black powder coat. But those arms held a mil-spec SA-13 assault rifle. Stolen and illegal, natch.

His defensive options were also far better than I was offered, and Slick wore a thick Sevenex bullet-stopper vest under his sleeveless leather jacket. Fluid-backed obliterative nanofiber – soft armor that turned bullets into liquid and vapor when they hit. Also stolen.

"There's our little bunny nest," he grinned, flashing a few teeth.

Do bunnies have nests? I skipped it and stretched to glance over his shoulder. Against the far back corner of the warehouse, someone had stacked a dozen metal cargo containers to make a walled compound. There were a few streamers of light stabbing out from seams and openings in the stack.

"Oh, that's cute," I whispered. "They built themselves a little fort."

Our target had to be there since the rest of the warehouse was pretty barren. But I supposed we could have been working with bad intel. The light *could* just be from some homeless squatters getting wasted on two-credit liquor.

This was what drones like Bugger were made for. I pulled him from my backpack, snapped his little wings open, and tossed him up in the air.

The drone immediately connected to my NUI, feeding me his point of view through a small window in the corner of my vision. I thought about flying over to the stack of crates, and Bugger responded, silently gliding to the objective.

Slick didn't bother waiting for me to report my findings. He darted off in a crouch toward the container fort and disappeared into the shadows.

I hung back, guiding Bugger around the fort. No sign of gun-toting gangers yet, so I parked him in the air near the containers and started creeping ahead.

Unlike Slick, I made sure to stick to the shadows rather than making myself an open target. My own wetgear was, again, hand-me-down ganger junk, and sure as hell wasn't wrapped in Sevenex. My arm and leg weren't even old-school Kevlar. But they did let me walk and juggle, two things I was not ready to do out of the womb. You take what you can get.

I made it halfway to the fort by way of various junkpiles before the warehouse erupted in a deafening roar of automatic rifle fire. The sound echoed off the surrounding steel walls so many times over I couldn't tell where it was coming from, but there were definitely a lot of muzzle flashes around the containers.

"Eat shit!" someone yelled, barely audible over the crackle of weapons fire.

Slick was already making friends.

With bullets flying, I had little to contribute beyond moral support. But I needed to earn my bond points and wouldn't get any if Slick was dead. Or if he decided I didn't pull my weight, he could cut me down from the full payout.

I drew my knife and ran around the backside of the cargo fort, hoping that Slick's piss-poor aim wouldn't pop a hole in me.

Other than wishing I had a plasma cartridge for my knife so I could cut through the side of one of those containers, I had no actual clue what to do. The gunfire slowed down from a constant roar to staccato bursts, but the sound of ricochets on metal were still too close to give me room to improvise.

Hell, I didn't even know where the hostile fire was coming from. Inside a container? Someone on top? Had I seen anyone while I was creeping my way over here? Skitz, I really didn't thrive in chaos. At least I could tell where Slick was by his muzzle flashes and shouted obscenities.

"Somebody kill that Lucky trash!" a different voice echoed *way* too close to where I was sneaking.

More gunfire, more ricochets.

Then, like a gift from above, a rifle clattered to the warehouse floor directly at my feet. It was followed by a massive dude with a fully-geared torso and a bloody meat stump where his head should have been. His corpse belly-flopped on top of the rifle with a metallic thud.

"Okay," I said, "someone *was* on top of the containers."

Slick's spray-and-pray method paid off, but he hadn't hit the jackpot yet. The exchange of gunfire continued, and now I could make out a few voices inside the fort. They sounded scared. I sheathed my knife and cracked my knuckles. Time to earn those points.

It took considerable effort to push the dead guy out of the way, but I managed to grab his rifle from underneath him. There was slippery blood all over it, but I was able to open the chamber to make sure it was still loaded. The rifle was no SA-13, but it could sling lead, so at that moment, I loved it.

I shouldered the weapon and worked my way around the front of the fort, being sure to take the route that Slick was *not* firing toward.

More bursts, more ricochets, more swearing. Either Slick was really, really bad with his aim, or that fort was packed deep with ganger gunslingers.

Finally, I found some footholds welded into the side of one of the containers. Hanging the rifle from my shoulder by its sling, I climbed up slowly and peeked over the top.

A pair of moving shadows came into view. Two targets on the far edge of the fort, shooting away from me and being generally oblivious of my presence.

"Slick," I thought, pinging him on my neurocom. "Stop shooting for a sec."

"What? No," his rough voice sounded in my head.

"You chungus, I need to get up top, and I don't want you hitting me!"

He laughed so hard I could hear it echoing through the warehouse in realspace.

"Alright, make it quick, girl. You got until I reload."

I slipped over the top of the container and crouched. With a conscious effort to steady my breathing, I shouldered the rifle, leveled the sights, and tried not to think about how little experience I had firing hot steel.

Squeezing the trigger twice, I leaned into the recoil. Then the blinding muzzle flash and ringing in my ears put me off balance. I staggered and blinked before realizing that there was still a chorus of gunfire tearing through the warehouse.

Guess I missed.

Half blind – and now even less confident in my skills at gunplay – a sudden compulsion to dive back down from the containers overcame me. I flung myself to the floor and landed on my ass, the rifle clattering down beside me.

Spots in my eyes didn't stop me from seeing through Bugger's camera, so I pulled that window back into focus. Through his overhead POV, I could see the two gangers – one was now moving across the top of the fort toward me.

Another chance to follow my instincts. I steered Bugger directly toward the closest goon's face at top speed.

My POV window provided an excellent hi-res look up the guy's nose right before the drone smashed into his face. I heard a 'clunk', then saw the man stumble off the top of the container fort and land on his head.

Didn't think that would work, honestly.

Bugger was flying a bit wonky after the hit, so maneuvering him around to take a run at the second gunslinger wasn't going as well. It felt more like guiding a one-eyed chicken to a pile of corn than a falcon's precision dive-bomb attack.

Left, right, left, hold it steady…

Finally, I connected Bugger's nose with the back of the gunner's head. And the drone sort of just bounced off.

"What the hell?" his voice echoed above me.

The gunslinger turned and raised up his rifle to slap Bugger out of the air next to him.

Then his head exploded in time with a volley of shots from Slick's rifle. I was able to make out that much before the flying goo covered Bugger's camera, and the drone fell into a nosedive.

Disconnected. Crap.

"You see that shot?" Slick's voice broke the silence in my head. "Zeroed 'em good. Anyone else alive over there?"

I waited. Listened. The warehouse seemed even darker now after cracking off those rounds, but I couldn't see any movement in either the shadows or the small slivers of light inside the fort.

"I think we're clear," I reported.

"I'm comin' over there, Jackie. And you better not have a piece in your hands."

I had no desire to pick that bloody rifle back up. I was more concerned about my drone. It took a few minutes of searching the shadows to find Bugger on the ground with a broken wing.

"There you are," I sighed. "You did good."

At least the damage looked fixable. I picked him up and carefully returned him to my backpack.

Slick came around the corner and gave me a flat look. Whether it was appreciation or anger, I had no clue. At least he didn't try to smile at me.

"This must be the way in," he said, pointing his rifle toward a container with its doors facing out toward us. He kicked the latch open and stepped in.

There were strings of LED lights woven throughout the inside of the container fort, not entirely bright but much better than outside in the warehouse bay. There were also a lot of fresh bullet holes in the containers.

"Dammit," I said, catching myself from falling, "so many casings and blood puddles I can't walk in here."

"Ha," Slick chuckled. "I jacked this place up. The mark's probably popped through and bled out by now."

I noticed that his leather jacket had a few new holes, too. If not for his bullet stopper vest, *he'd* have been popped through and bleeding out.

We found five dead gangers on the fort's floor, but none was the target. Then we spotted a container welded over with steel panels and secured with a heavy padlock. Slick pointed to a series of cables and tubes running to the back of the container.

"Yahtzee," he grinned.

I knew what was coming and stepped back. My handheld 'facer couldn't do much about caveman tech like an analog padlock, but Slick's kickass weapon – made by the same corp that makes my knife, thank you – had an integrated 'master key' system under the rifle barrel. A quick blast from that scaled-down, lock-shredding shotgun had the door open in less than a second.

"There she is," Slick rasped, pulling both door flaps open.

Yup, there she was. The target was a rival gang's brainer, a fully-spec'd out human CPU, sitting completely still and silent in a NetOps chair. The implants in her skull were connected to a bunch of data cables, but it was the coolant flowing through tubes running into her head that I noticed first. The purple liquid caught so much light that even in the dimness of the container fort it seemed to glow.

"Check out the monitor. She's alive," I said.

"Not for long. Do her, and let's roll."

I gave Slick a dirty look. Brainers were ultra-valuable, but it was too risky to try to capture one. The policy was to take the head and leave the rest since the neural implants were worth more credits than the biobag wearing them anyway.

But it's one thing to fight, even if you're just doing it to pay off your bond debt. But this...was definitely straight-up murder.

"Come on, Jack. It's barely a human at this point. Sittin' there mining the blockchain or whatever the hell it's doin'."

He had a point. Once you became a brainer, you spent the rest of your life strapped into a chair. You were an appliance – and I had no idea why people chose that particular career.

Unsheathing my knife, I stepped toward the girl with all her wires and tubes. For the most part, she looked like any teenager who'd fallen asleep in a chair. After shaving off all their hair, I guess. She might as well have been me.

"Oh for shit's sake," Slick pushed past me and snatched my knife from my hand.

Before I could so much as gasp, he'd buried the blade in the girl's neck. With a few sawing cuts, her head dropped from the chair, hanging only by its wires and tubes. Somewhere behind me, a monitor was buzzing an alert.

"Bag that up, and let's skid. I gotta decide if I'm going to deduct points from your sorry ass."

For not following orders, he meant. For hesitating about...

Ugh. Fewer points meant I'd have to do even more jobs before my debt was paid in full. It was a very real threat, and I was sure any bonuses I'd earned by helping to flatline two rival gangers had just gone down the toilet.

Slick stepped out of the container while I removed my large pack from my back and zipped it open. I doubt it was designed to carry severed heads, but it *was* waterproof.

Unplugging the dangling head was downright offensive to the senses.

The worst thing, though? Slick hadn't given my knife back.

Chapter Two

BAD MEMORIES

Lugging that brainer's head from the warehouse got me thinking. Mostly about how weird it was that this was my life, and how months of doing skitz like this had already gone by.

A year ago, I was pretty normal for a Hope Megacity kid. Smart, I was told. But isolated thanks to my handicaps.

I'd been born with…issues. Defects in my nervous system meant I had to go right from the womb to life support. The next day, my left arm and right leg were amputated due to complications.

BioDyne stepped in and offered to put me – little baby Jack – into an alpha test program. They'd sort out all of my nervous system issues with experimental implants. Mom and dad just had to sign some waivers – and agree to pay for it.

I was hanging on the edge of death from the first second I entered the world. It wasn't much of a choice for a parent.

But it cost them hundreds of thousands in BioDyne corporate scrip. More than both of them would make in ten years. So it was taken on as debt to the 'generous' corporation that saved baby girl Jack. Payments came out of mom's salary. Until there wasn't a salary.

Anyway, none of that helped with the missing arm and leg. I stayed home a lot. I'd read from my terminal and learn about tech. Part of me hoped that I would find some broken wetgear in the trash some day and fix it. Replace my own missing limbs, you know?

It just got worse after mom died from silverlung. I was thirteen. Dad did all the work on his own after that while I focused on my education. He managed to keep it all going until I graduated.

But when I turned eighteen, it all came crashing down. Hanska Construction was about to terminate his contract and send his debt to collections. If he didn't want the debt to carry over to me, he would have to enlist in a voluntary servitude program. A *twenty-year* program. And they could ship him anywhere in the world to work his debt off as a laborer.

So he did. It left me with no prospects and a tiny apartment paid for by his contract – and I was still short two appendages. I don't blame him. If anything, I know how much I owe him. It was *my* medical bills that forced him to sell his soul to corpos.

And now I'm carrying a head in a bag.

That means I learned two things from dad: a love of figuring out machines, and a propensity for signing shitty deals.

It was good to remember this stuff. I thought about it every time I finished a job because it kept things in perspective. Bloody heads didn't matter. Slick's body odor didn't matter.

I needed to get away from the Luckies, and I needed to buy back dad's soul. That's what mattered, so that's what I focused on while climbing into our busted sedan's passenger seat.

Slick got behind the wheel, and fired up the engine.

Chapter Three

THE LUCKIES

The ride back to the gang's HQ was as quiet as the severed head in my lap – until Slick started grumbling about driving anything that wasn't a motorcycle, then cranked up some ultra-hard roadcore track.

That was about the depth of his conversation skills, but I was so pissed about the op that I was okay with him blasting music rather than trying to talk to me.

The funny thing was that the bio-neural hardware attached to the brainer's head was easily worth ten times the wetgear I was trying to pay off. Even the cheapest brainer implants were top-shelf tech.

My left arm and leg were mid-grade even before they were used and abused. And who knows where the Luckies got them before they sold them to me.

I stared out the window to get my mind off of it. It was still early, but the sidewalks were already crammed with people on their way to wherever. We were driving through the worst part of the Quarters, so they were probably on their way to beg or get pissed drunk on vending machine liquor.

A few of them might have had jobs in the factories that weren't closed down and falling apart in this district, but they mostly didn't look like people with responsibilities. Like so many people in the city, they looked like half-living zombos.

Some people give up, some people fight, and some people win. That was the class structure of the entire world. Outside the window were the shambling masses that gave up. In the front seat, banging his head to the worst possible music, was someone who fights.

And the people who win? They didn't live down here with the scrappers, druggos, gangers, workers, and dregs. They live above the clouds in HighHold. A whole kingdom on SkyPillar legs, thousands of feet above our sprawling Hope Megacity.

What could we do about it? Not a damn thing. That's why I was cruising the worst district in the mega with a bloodied head on my lap. But hey, the Luckies' HQ was just ahead, so at least the ride was almost over.

Slick jammed the brakes beside the two-story abandoned apartment building, the base of the 204th Avenue Luckies in all its splendor. Truth be told, it was just a brick building with an entire wall covered by a faded billboard.

Through years of accumulated grime and bird crap, I could barely make out the big, blue letters. They read 'Welcome to the New City of Hope!', with two similar lines beneath in Arabic and Spanish. A relic from the first few years after the city was built. Back when the founders shuttled people here from all over the planet.

Over ten million people, they say. All of them volunteers who wanted to escape the chaos and death of the rest of the world.

This district was where they first arrived. Quarantine, processing, and immigrant quartering – hence the name. And the walls that are still around it. After the population project ended around seventy years ago, the corpos let the whole district fall apart.

Now, the Luckies' HQ was a shining example of the Quarters' aesthetic. Rough, unkempt, and surrounded by trash and debris. The only thing clean within five blocks was the gang's row of black-on-chrome Corley road bikes in the alley.

Slick shut off the car and jumped out. I was right behind him with my backpack in hand.

We reported directly to Monk as soon as we got in the building. Monk was the lieutenant in charge of this particular chapter and the only Lucky I'd ever seen who didn't have any wetgear prosthetics of any kind.

The rest of the gangers around us were decked out to some degree in the Luckies' trademark flat-black cybernetics. Even the members who couldn't afford lifelike casings and powder coating would spraypaint their naked gear with rattle cans.

Not Monk. He had the usual neurocom and interfacing implants in his skull, but all his limbs and organs were straight-up stock, birth-issued meat.

What he *did* have was a crapload of ink. His muscle-slab of a body was tattooed from his shaved head to his feet with roses, barbed wire, swords, skulls, swallows, and damn near anything else you could find on a tattooist's wall. Of course, the most important tat was the huge pair of dice showing two sevens covering his right cheek – the mark of the Luckies.

I had to look at those tattoos a lot since I became bonded to them a year ago, and it always bothered me that their six-sided dice had sevens. Whatever. A small thing to put up with when you're carrying a human head.

"Yo, Slick," Monk said as we approached. "Looks like you got it."

He traded a macho arm-grab gesture with Slick and then held out his hand to me. There was a spider tattooed on his palm.

"Give it here. Let's see it."

I tossed Monk the backpack, and he dumped it over the table in front of him. The head bounced among the empty beer bottles and dirty ashtrays on the table and set them rattling.

"Alriiiiight!" he said, laughing. "Double win. A Santos brainer off the grid and some next-level wetgear to take to the chop."

Monk scooped the head off the table and lobbed it over to a Lucky in full black leathers who'd just walked into the room.

"Get that over to Dicky, brother. Tell him we want no less than 20 stacks for that skitz. Upfront."

The other ganger nodded and about-faced through the door, tucking the head under his arm to fire up a smoke.

"So let's talk points." Monk flashed a grin right at me. "How'd our little Jackie do on this one?"

I hated when people called me that. That a-hole wouldn't want me calling him 'Monkie', but when you're dealing with someone who's more ink than skin, you have to pick your battles.

"One door hack," Slick answered while flopping down on a ripped couch.

He kicked his feet up on an upturned ammunition crate before adding that I'd taken out a 9th Street goon with a drone the size of a street taco. Although he didn't explain it in quite as flattering a way.

"Racking up kills?" Monk laughed. "You tryin' to earn your ink, so you can ride with the Luckies all official?"

"Not really," I replied. "I never learned how to ride a motorcycle, so...not much of a fit."

Monk and Slick both laughed even though it wasn't a joke. I didn't want my ink. I didn't want to be a ganger for the rest of my life. And I really didn't know how to ride a bike.

"Hell, girl, we can teach you how to ride," Monk continued. "What we can't teach is how to be a cold-blooded soldier. That's bred in the bone, and it's startin' to look like you got it."

"Thanks," was all I could muster before he continued talking.

"Tell you what. You owe us...let's see...236 more points. That's at least five more jobs."

"Maybe ten if there's cockups," Slick added before taking a swig of beer.

"Yeah, yeah. But how 'bout this, Jack. One more job, a big one. Zero the rest of the points. Then we talk about bringing you in."

Slick chuckled. "Pft. I'm not teaching her skinny ass how to ride."

Monk froze for a split second as if his brain was buffering. I'd known the man for over a year now, in that time watching him slide down a rabbit hole of reckless overindulgence – chems and stims, mostly. They made him quicker on his feet, and physically stronger, but moments like this threw a spotlight on the toll it was having on his mind.

"You will if I fuckin' say you will," he growled, pointing a meaty finger right in Slick's face. "You read me?"

Slick put his hands up and sank into the couch, grin thoroughly deleted. Watching a one-hundred-percent organic man stare down a guy with two wetgear arms that could snap a graphene rod in half was quite a thing. I guess even Slick knew about picking battles, and he was the biggest smoothbrain I'd ever met.

"Goddammit," said Monk, cracking his neck and turning back to me. "You ruined a solemn moment here, Slick. Anyway, let's hear it, Jack. You takin' this deal or what?"

I really did not want to be a 204th Avenue Lucky. Ugh. To think of having to see those stupid dice showing sevens every time I looked in the mirror.

But to have my debt cleared? I might not survive five or ten more jobs, so skipping to the end of the story might be the only way out. But only if they let me go without branding me into their gang. If I could pull that off, I'd be shiny.

I decided it was time to roll the dice, though even thinking in that metaphor made my stomach turn.

THE LAST JOB

I was on my way less than an hour later.

Monk and I worked out a solid deal, but I couldn't shake the feeling that something wasn't right about it.

According to the meatslab, I was getting my debt cleared for doing a big job, but this didn't seem like a big job. It was barely a job at all. It was a pickup and delivery that any gig worker with the Fetchem app could have done.

The fact that it didn't seem worth *two* points, much less two hundred, meant that something dangerous was going on that I wasn't privy to.

Then again, it may have just been a task that required discretion. It was hard for Luckies to go unseen thanks to their facial tattoos and black cybernetics. And all the studded leather. And loud motorcycles.

Shit, they *really* weren't discrete.

Anyway, I didn't have much choice. I'd taken the deal – knowing that I would have to weasel out of the gang initiation later – and there I was, on the metro headed toward my contact with a "valuable package" nestled next to Bugger, the drone, in my backpack. At least it wasn't a head this time.

That was after a long walk out of the Quarters. The district had very little to offer to anyone other than a squatter or druggo, including rail stations or cab terminals. Freelance unFare drivers wouldn't even do pick-ups for fear of being shanked or carjacked, plus getting through the gates was just an unnecessary hassle.

I didn't mind the walk. Like most things in the world, most of the fear about the Quarters was a bunch of BS. Sure, dregs and opt-outs were at the bottom of the social ladder, but they didn't run around knifing and robbing everyone that moved. They were people with no scrip, no status, mental problems, that sort of thing – and to the corporations, that made them *not* people. Since the corpos control the narrative, well, you get the idea.

There *were* the gangs, natch. But the district was big enough that they could avoid each other when they wanted to. Hell, the Quarters was bigger than some places that used to be called cities two hundred years ago.

After leaving the blocks of shanties, gutted buildings, and junk piles, I went to the metro station on the edge of Palace Park. That meant passing through a police checkpoint at the wall cutting the Quarters off from the rest of the mega. I'd managed to keep myself free of a criminal record, so that was cake.

From Palace Park, I rode the underground rail to the far edge of Hope Megacity. Urban sprawl being what it was, that ride took nearly an hour.

I got off the train in Camden Cay, a major shipping district at the edge of the mega where air traffic was dominated by 300-foot-long cargo airships. Big bastards that used vacuum buoyancy and directed thrust motors to do the work of old-world ships without a need for oceans. They were the whole reason this megacity could be built in the most landlocked part of the continent instead of on a coast, like most Pre-Collapse cities.

Walking back up to street level was like stepping into an entirely different world. Where I'd boarded at Palace Park was all trees, animal holograms, and water features. That district was surrounded by some of the most expensive 45-story condos in the mega. Now I exited into the blurry line between the airharbor and a massive low-status neighborhood.

With the sun low in the sky, the overcity cast its shadow over the district. The wind carried mist and tiny droplets of rain from the east – rain fell almost constantly from HighHold's bed of engineered clouds.

Only the central districts directly beneath the overcity felt the brunt of it, and Camden Cay was one of the most western districts on the outskirts of Hope. Just like in the Quarters, I could see the sky overhead. An open street market with dozens of stalls crammed beneath strings of paper lanterns sprawled out to my left. To my right, a wall of cargo cranes and container stacks stood silhouetted against the setting sun. The entire scene was loud, with talking and shouting and pedestrians blasting music, and the air around the skyharbor smelled like airship fuel and electricity.

Every surface was covered with advertising, whether a holo, vid screen, or printed poster – all in a mix of English, Arabic, and Spanish. On top of that was the usual layer of grime, spit, and whatever else accumulated in low-status neighborhoods.

I adjusted my backpack on my shoulder because it was, as they say, time for business.

I had to find a streethawk named Gina somewhere near the club that sponsored her. She would lead me to another contact, and I'd trade the package for an isostick containing a very flush crypto wallet.

I didn't know much about what I was handing off. It was definitely an old-school solid-state drive inside a ruggedized case, but Monk had only said it was a 'cash cow' for whoever had it.

Course he also told me he'd break my organic leg and repo my gear if I tried to run off with it. That's to be expected, but what I found puzzling was how a bunch of skeez bikers who made all their money through protection and guns had gotten hold of valuable data.

Not my circus, so I put it out of my head and walked toward the market's neon signs.

The scene was typical of a lower-class evening in Hope. Vendors hawking meat on sticks. Cheap clothes and jewelry hanging from other stalls. Groups of young nightcrawlers gathered around speakers or sat on steps slinging back bottles and cans.

A little pang of envy kicked in. I hadn't gotten the chance to sit around idle for that long in my life. Once I'd escaped the sponsored brainwashing of the school system, I looked for ways to get wetgear replacements for my absentee arm and leg. It took months of asking around, but eventually the Luckies took a shine to my tech skills. Bing, boom, new arm and leg. The year that followed was nothing but doing jobs for Monk to pay them off.

And even with my final job right in front of me, I didn't see a vacation in my future. I wouldn't be crashing at the Lucky HQ and eating their food any more. The upside was I wouldn't need to dodge Monk's advances either, but I would need to find a way to earn my own crypto. And it would take a *lot* of scrip to buy my father's freedom.

The crowd got thicker as I moved deeper into the street market. The mingled mess looked like it stretched on for at least six more blocks.

"My bad," a girl with pink hair and a nice pair of synthskin legs giggled as she bumped past me.

More envy, this time for those long wetgear legs curving down from her miniskirt. The goldish carbon fiber casing of my limbs sure didn't pass for human skin. Not like hers. At least the Luckies hadn't held me down and painted my cybernetics black to match theirs.

I pushed past a vendor selling bootleg cinema cartridges, another with racks of neon-colored shirts and printed hats, all while keeping my eyes open for my contact's club – Cloud Seven.

The name made me think the place was definitely a front for the Luckies. I'd bet my organic arm that Gina was 'affiliated' with someone in the Camden chapter of the gang.

After squeezing my way through a hundred Hope Mega denizens, I finally spotted the sign. It bore a raunchy depiction of a bent-over woman with a white-neon cloud covering her parts. Underneath, flickering letters spelled out "CLOUD 7".

I just had to find Gina, and the crowd was no thinner around the sex club. Since she was a streethawk, a living advertisement for the club, I figured she should be somewhere within eyeshot of the front door. At least Monk had given me a thoroughly inadequate description of the girl. 'Short blue hair and a nice rack' described at least thirty people in my line of sight at that moment.

Finally, I saw her. A girl with short blue hair, looked about nineteen, and flirting with people passing by. She checked all the boxes, so I pushed my way through the crowd toward her.

"Gina?" I asked.

She looked me over, and a row of perfect, white teeth peeked through her blue lipstick. "Herself. And you're Jackie?"

"Ugh," I said flatly. "Jack. Just Jack."

Gina snickered and apologized. "Monk told me to call you that. He has a thing for you, you know."

I was all too aware. Honestly, I was never wanting for attention at the Luckies' HQ – and by that I mean I didn't want all the attention I got. Monk was just the worst about laying off, but plenty of others tried.

"I don't blame him, you're pretty," she said with a wry grin. "I'll bet you could get a club to take you on. Cloud Seven would take you in a hot minute."

"Nah, not that I'm against...any of this. It's just not my thing."

"Think about it, girl. After you work the street team for a while, you get some really nice gear. Synthskin, new eyes, voice mods, poofy tail. There's a market for all of it in there."

"I'm still paying off these floor models," I said, raising my arm. Although I did wonder what I would look like with a poofy tail.

Nah.

Gina shrugged and made a soft cooing noise. She was definitely cute, and I figured it wouldn't take her long to be promoted to...an hourly position...inside the club. I thought about telling her she didn't need any cyber mods to turn heads, but I'd be wasting my time. People didn't become clubtoys because they wanted to run stock hardware. They were attracted to the showiness of it all.

"Speaking of my crushing debts," I went on, "you're supposed to point me toward...you know..."

"Yup. Go down that alley, and turn right at the broken Chug machine. There's a door with the number 23 on it. Go in there." She dug her slender fingers into her bra and pulled out an old-school keycard. "Use this to get in."

I took the keycard and shoved it into my pocket.

"And my buyer person is in there? Room 23?"

"I guess so," she said with genuine innocence that didn't fit the scenery. "They don't tell me much."

"Alright. Thanks, Gina," I smiled and tossed my long hair over my shoulder, though I'm not sure why I'd made the extra gesture.

"Bye, baby girl!" she beamed and waved her fingers.

Before getting two steps away, Gina was already back to cooing and flirting with the men and women walking by. Her job was to get them into the club to see the *better* attractions. Considering her top-shelf looks, I found the idea of there being better attractions fairly intimidating.

I smiled when I realized I was still twirling a strand of my hair in my fingers.

A few more steps down the alley and the Chug machine was there, as promised, busted open and hollowed out in the shadows. I took the next right and activated the fingertip flashlight on my wetgear hand to cut through the encroaching darkness.

I had to step over piles of trash and discarded junk to make my way from door to door but eventually made it to the marked entrance without tripping over anything. Kicking aside a dead rat, I moved closer to swipe the keycard.

"Hold up," a man's voice came from the shadows behind me, and I almost peed my favorite leggings.

Spinning on my heel, I aimed my glowing fingertip into the darkness. The beam of white light landed on a clean-cut guy in a full three-piece corpo suit.

"Skitz, dude," I said. "Did I kick that rat on you? My bad…"

"No, you didn't, Jack. I'm here for the package."

Ooooh, *the package*. The guy was so formal.

Even though this was my first solo job, I'd tagged along on enough ops to have some idea of how they usually played out. I ask to see the thing they have, then I show them the thing I have, then we trade things, and we go our separate ways.

Maybe it *wasn't* so different from being a clubtoy? I went to slide my bag off my shoulder, but the suit stopped me.

"Not here," he said. "I've got a room this way."

So much for going our separate ways. I wasn't too thrilled about having to follow a corpo creeper deeper into a dark alley – and I would never have if it wasn't going to clear my bond debt – but I fell in behind him.

Then I noticed that his close-cropped corpo haircut was shaved away to accommodate a neural implant at the base of his skull. He was prolly a psycher, decked out for jacking directly into the DarkNet.

I didn't know that much about the practice firsthand. It wasn't the kind of thing that made it into ganger circles very often – too expensive and too high of a skill requirement. I just knew that psychers got themselves wired up sort of like a brainer, but didn't go so far as becoming a vegetable in a NetOps chair.

Seeing how the guy was a corpo *and* a psycher, I was feeling less and less sure of what kind of outcome to expect.

All I could think about was how much it sucked that Slick had taken my blade, my one defensive tool. I mean, I could throw a decent punch with my wetgear arm, but it wasn't the sort of model that shatters rib cages when you need to fend off a weirdo.

Oh well.

I followed the suit all the way out of the alley, down the block, and into a small motel that took up the first few floors of a high-rise apartment building. It wasn't the seediest place I'd ever seen, but it sure made the list. We took the stairs up to the third floor, passed a couple of broken monitors on the landings, and then the suit swiped his hand on the door of room thirty-six. Even the door's staticky access beep sounded like it didn't want to be there.

Once inside the tiny room, he stood on the far side of a small round table in the corner, all dressed and pressed. Compared to the leather, mohawk, non-bathing set that I'd grown used to, this guy was damn near a movie star. He was about as handsome as one, too.

As soon as I walked closer, he threw something heavy on the table in front of me. A carbon fiber wallet with a gold inlay. It was a badge engraved with the insignia of the largest net security corporation on the planet. Damn.

"Overwatch?" I said. "What the hell?"

"Don't freak," he said, holding out his hand. "First off, you're not in trouble. Like I told you, I'm here to make a deal."

"Wait, you're the buyer? Naaaah. Monk's greedy, but I don't see him doing deals with a corpo."

"I am, and I'm not," he said, grinning. "My name is Associate Mikael Goodwin. I'm here to make a deal with *you*. I don't like screwing around any more than you do, so I'll lay this out first: I know you're not a lowlife ganger, Jacqueline. Your loyalty only goes as far as paying off what you owe. I also know that you're very eager to get your father out of corporate servitude."

"What the fu…"

Goodwin raised his hand and my words trailed off.

"I can tell you're getting angry," he continued, "but hear me out. I'm not trying to give you a hard time. I'm offering you a way out. You do us a favor, and we'll pay for your father's release."

It was one hell of an offer. The best I could figure, it was going to take me years to save up enough credits to buy out his servitude contract. And that was assuming I could find paid work any time soon.

"And what about my debt to the Luckies?"

"Well, Jack, I'll put it this way. If you do us this favor, the Luckies will no longer be anyone's problem, including yours."

Chapter Five

THE BARGAIN

S weat beaded on my forehead while I listened to Goodwin's deal. Was it too good to be true or just a load of corporate BS?

"If you tell me you're on board with this," he said, "I get to go back to the office and give my bosses good news. You get your father back for the first time in years. You're free of the Luckies forever. Hell, if what I've heard about your techie skills is true, I might even be able to get you a job where you won't have to sleep in rat holes like this for the rest of your life."

His gesture implied that 'rat holes' descriptor applied to far more than just the confines of the motel room. Sighing, I processed the thought. The deal didn't matter – I just needed to remember who was offering it.

I stopped chewing the inside of my cheek and shot him a frown. "First off, this place is nicer than where I've been sleeping for the last year. Second, I just...can't trust you. I don't know a thing about you other than that you have a badge. And that makes me trust you even less."

The suit smiled, picked his badge off the table, and put it back in his jacket pocket.

"I'm not totally blind to your situation. 'Corporations are the enemy. Corporations are the one-percent'. I get it. I wasn't born upstairs. I wasn't even born in New Leeds or Palace Park. You know where I'm from? Right here. I grew up in a shitty apartment two blocks east. I shared a bed with two brothers until I was fourteen."

He had my attention, even though my instinct was to build walls around every word he said.

"I'll never be in the one-percent, Jack. But I'm also not looking through trash bins for food or waking up every morning to the smell of airship fuel and failure. Sometimes choosing sides isn't about principles. It's about surviving."

He pointed at my cybernetic arm.

"I don't need to tell you that, do I? We both threw our lots in where we had to so we could get what we needed. And this...this is just your chance to throw in with people who can give you more than some refurbished wetgear and a face tattoo."

God help me if Associate Goodwin wasn't making sense. I wasn't loyal to the Luckies – I didn't even like them. So if I was going to use people to get what I wanted, why not use a corporation with limitless resources?

And – bonus – I wouldn't have to worry about dodging the gang initiation.

"Alright, *associate*. Let's start with the favor. What am I supposed to do?"

Goodwin nodded his approval before pulling a slate from under the table and switching on the screen.

He showed me a few images and reports while explaining that the 'cash cow' in my backpack was crypto-mining tech stolen from Omni Financial. The Luckies weren't behind the heist; they were only hired to fence the tech to the highest bidder. Goodwin didn't explain who *did* steal the tech, but the names ARGO, Rosewhite, and Zoroaster kept flashing by in the reports. I'd never heard of any of them.

"And Monk didn't tell you everything about this deal we set up," he continued. "You're not trading the tech for credits, you're trading it for a top-shelf network infiltration app. As far as the Luckies know, this software is ripped straight from the Overwatch servers and worth millions."

"Yeah, but there is no app, right? You just want the tech back."

"Oh, there's an app, Jack. This is where the favor comes in." Goodwin pulled a small case from his jacket.

"You bring this isostick back to the Luckies. When one of them pops this in their neurocom port to verify it, it'll inject a very aggressive tracking bug. This is an opportunity to leverage their lack of tech-savvy and get our eyes on a vast network of bad guys."

"Entire network, huh? How is your bug gonna spread that far?"

"It's self-propagating, so it'll spread from vector zero to their neurocom contacts, social accounts, and anyone within MiFi range. It's all run by a bleeding-edge algorithm, so it's not completely indiscriminate about who it tracks, but it's damn fast."

"Yeah, that sounds pretty aggressive."

"Before you ask, you've been whitelisted. It won't touch you. And for the people it does infiltrate, we just want their locations and movements so HMPD can round them up. No reason this needs to get any darker than that."

"How does that protect me when they realize I botched this sale? Monk will rip my head off as soon as he sees the software isn't real."

"He won't know. The tracker's buried under a fake UI. It looks real enough for someone who doesn't know what they're doing, so you'll have plenty of time to get gone after the exchange. We'll extract you at the edge of the Quarters and keep you under our protection until all the arrests have been made."

It was all adding up. I had to admit that for all their evils, corporations were very good at planning. I was used to doing half-assed jobs with Slick, and here was an operation laid out so smoothly you could skate on it.

Associate Goodwin spent the next hour running me through the rest of the plan. What to say, where to go for my extraction, and what would happen to me after the op. He even zipped me the contact deets for an Overwatch recruiter.

"You're doing a great thing," he said, leading me out the door. "For yourself and for your father."

He didn't mention that the corporations would benefit more than anyone. But I guess that was always a given.

Things after leaving the motel were a bit of a dull blur. It was a lot to take in, so I stared into one of the news monitors on the metro ride back to Park Palace.

The news was always pretty easy to zonk out to. Currency reports. Corporate press conferences. On-the-scene footage of protests and riots was always on the menu, but it was a sure bet the reporter would slant toward defending the corps even when people were being hosed down with tear gas in the street. Or bullets, if it was a big enough protest.

> "...live footage from the Eurasia front as NEU forces overwhelm Chinese strongpoints in the former Ukraine. In other news, BioDyne has announced the approval of Retovicol II, stating that the nanodrug can now reverse the symptoms of silverlung in over ninety-four percent of cases..."

About fifteen years too late to save mom, BioDyne. When I was eight, she contracted silverlung from working in a nanotech production lab. That was before they knew nanites were getting into people's lungs and turning the tissue into aluminum foil. To no one's surprise, the lab she worked in was owned by none other than BioDyne.

Corporations made a lot of money selling solutions to problems they caused.

> "...exciting new development from TaoCom Global as they prepare to unveil a new means of instantaneous transportation. CEO Ren Xie proudly stated that the new tech will revolutionize everything from international travel to deep space exploration. At eleven, we'll talk to Hope Megacity mayoral candidate Aaren Hamid about the growing accusations of collusion regarding the 2158 drinking water scandal..."

Listening to the news always made me feel like there was so much of nothing going on. It was always the same things happening in cycles. Enough to make me wonder why we even bother if the wheel just keeps turning back to the same place. Rich people are happy. Poor people starve. Politicians suck. Armies kill each other. Really...how was any of that *news*?

The train began to slow, and a speaker crackled to life over my head.

> "Stand by for Palace Park station. Thank you for enjoying Hope Metro Rail!"

'Enjoying' was a bit of a stretch. Maybe if they dialed down the pee smell on their trains a notch.

I left the station and made the long walk back through the Quarters' checkpoint and to the front door of the Luckies' headquarters.

When I'd left the motel, I was only half enticed by promises of a better life. Now I was looking at the rathole where I'd been living for the last year with fresh eyes. It was horrible. I did deserve better. And to hell with the gangers who ran me through so much crap for stupid bond points.

That was all about to end, and I finally felt like my life could improve. It was a bizarre feeling, like when you look over the side of a building and the street is so far down you can't even see the cars, and then you get that rush in your belly and a little surge of fear and excitement. And for a solid nanosecond, you feel like you could leap over the edge and watch the ground race toward you.

And it's not that you *want* to die like a street pancake. It's just that crazy sensation in the middle of your stomach that hits as strong as a drug.

Before I could punch my code into the entry controls, the door slid open to reveal Monk's smiling, tattooed face. Slick, Dodo, Murphy, and ten other Luckies were all gathered behind him.

"Jack!" Monk said, scooping me inside the building. "Tell me we're all fuckin' rich, baby!"

I held out my backpack, and Slick snatched it up. After digging out the agent's small case and popping out the inch-long isostick, he passed the prize over to his boss.

Monk slid the stick into the port at the base of his skull. His eyes glazed over and tiny blue lights flicked on inside his pupils. He was loading the software.

"Alright…" he said, eyes still glossy and glowing. "Yeah. Yeah. This looks good. Real good."

I realized my hands were balled into fists and my organic leg was shaking. More beads of sweat on my forehead. Damn…I tried to summon a bit of the old 'calm under pressure' spirit before someone called me out for looking nervous.

Deep breath, Jack.

Monk popped the isostick from his port and clapped me on the shoulder.

"Perfect, Jack. Fuckin' perfect."

I smiled as authentically as possible to cover the worried gust of air escaping from my lungs. Now the hard part – I needed to slip out of there and get to the edge of the district.

"Crack 'em open, boys and girls!" Monk called out to the rest of the gangers packed in the room. "We got two causes to celebrate. We're rich, and we're bringing Jackie here into the fold."

Skitz. I looked around for anyone wielding a tattoo gun. They wouldn't push the issue that fast, right? Nah, they had to get drunk first. Party first, business later.

But the walls were closing in on me, and I couldn't risk hanging around. I had to get out of there.

"Hell yeah," I grinned while inching toward the hallway. "I gotta pee first. Save me a beer."

Monk nodded. The rest of the crew was already slamming back bottles and passing around a tray of pills. Slipping out wouldn't be too hard. Most of the magnetic locks on the windows were busted, so climbing out was a solid option. I went to the bathroom at the back of the building, a spot far away from the partying.

Shutting the door behind me, I climbed up on the toilet. The window behind it wasn't locked, but it definitely wasn't sliding open easily. It was jammed with years of rust and grime – the Luckies' lack of maintenance concerns was an annoyance before, and now it might get me killed.

I pushed all of my weight upward into the window and it finally gave way. Wind rushed in and instantly coated my face with a fresh powdering of dust. I put my arm through and...

"What the shit?" a voice rasped behind me.

Turning around, Slick rushed toward me with a pissed-off look on his roadkill face. He grabbed me hard and pulled me down from the window.

"C'mon, Jack. You can't skid out on your own party..."

I struggled but might as well have been buried in cement. His wetgear grip was brutal, and he could rip my arm right off my shoulder if he wanted to. Looking around for options, I noticed Slick still had my MMK knife in his belt.

I grabbed the hilt, yanking the knife from his belt and stabbing the blade straight up into his chin in one quick movement. My heart raced as the blade buried up to the guard, and I waited to feel my arms tearing away from my body when his reflexes kicked in.

No? Phew.

Slick's eyes went dead, and his hands released. When I pulled the knife back out, he dropped to the floor like a bag of rocks.

"Skitz," I whispered, looking at the door, then at Slick.

No time to waste, I jumped back on the toilet and climbed out the window. My feet hit the ground outside the HQ, and I felt the first satisfying wave of freedom wash over me.

That's when everything went to hell.

I'd barely taken my first step away from the Luckies' HQ when my cybernetic leg gave out. Falling to the ground, I caught a mouthful of dead grass and dusty earth.

Alerts flashed across my eyeline, created by the neurocom wiring on my optic nerves.

Malicious code detected. Interface error. Neural lock-out.

What the fu...

What I saw was nothing compared to what I heard. From inside the HQ, the sound of the gangers drinking and grab-assing turned into screams of pain and cries for help. I resorted to crawling away from the building with one working arm and leg, but it was getting harder to see where I was crawling to. My eyes flashed with digital artifacts, and a headache kicked in so strong I thought my brains were going supernova.

I made my escape a few inches at a time while the screaming slowly died down behind me. Looking over my shoulder, I saw Monk stagger from the front door of the HQ, holding his bald head in his hands. A second later, he dropped to the ground.

Did *his* brains go supernova? Skitz.

No time to think about how it was probably all my fault. I focused on crawling, knowing that I had to get as far away from the building as I could. I kept going until I couldn't make it another inch. Then the instinct to curl up in a dark hole took over. I had to hide while I could still think and see enough to do it – and that wouldn't be long.

I spotted a pile of rusty metal sheets and figured I had to be at least one or two buildings away from the HQ. Too jacked up to tell for sure, but it would have to be good enough. Using my working arm to clear a path underneath the scrap, I wriggled into the pile and blacked out.

Chapter Six

ERROR

*** BIODYNE BIOS 2 / WARP ***

...

....

..............Neurosensory User Interface Loaded.

Initializing NeurOS v. 3.1.

File Integrity Check...FAILED

Restoring Backup(s)

Persistent Error(s) Detected: 3

Connecting to MiFi.........SUCCESS!

Loading Peripheral Drivers...BioDyne Corp. CG-1 (Arm /L)...BioDyne Corp. RFX-15 (Leg/R)...TaoCom 55X-Q CNS Puck (Spinal/C3)...SUCCESS!

Good Evening, Jacqueline!

Holy hell, my head hurt.

Ugh. I hated waking up to a freakin' update. With my NUI blasting my senses with loading screens, I figured I might as well just lay there and wait. But damn, what a headache. Was I hungover?

Wait, where was I? And what the hell was on top of me?

I opened my eyes and remembered that I'd buried myself under a pile of trash. Oh hell...then I remembered everything else. Slick's blood all over my arm. The screaming. Associate Goodwin, the prick.

I pushed myself out of the trash heap, overjoyed that all of my limbs were working again. Why my wetgear was back online was a low-priority concern. Gift horses and mouths. The more pressing issue was that it was now dark out, and I was possibly being hunted by the Luckies or Overwatch.

I had no idea how long I'd zonked out, but it didn't matter. I needed to put distance between me and the Luckies' HQ, so I bolted toward the edge of the district. Getting out of the Quarters was my only plan for now. Anyone could disappear in a crowd of a hundred million people.

The promise of anonymity was really the only benefit of heading that way. Hope Megacity's endless horizon of neon and holograms was no candle in a window welcoming weary travelers. It was the electric fires of hell beckoning every lost soul it could suck in. For all the ads and promises of pleasures and opportunity, it was just a livestock pen for the people who lived above it.

The one-percent, as Goodwin had called them. The people in the clouds, looking down from their mile-high towers. Corpos and their closest collaborators who divided the world up among themselves a long time ago.

On the skyline in front of me, the seven Skypillars dominated everything. The oldest, Hanska Tower, was built by the Hanska Construction Corporation as a proof of concept for the cement-composite printing technology that eventually gave them a worldwide monopoly on megacity construction.

Once that big bastard was dominating the skyline, all of the GCs – Global Corporations – had to have one. TaoCom, Greysen Security, HighCastle, BioDyne, Kingdom Husein... Then they connected them with mile-high sky bridges. More connections were added over time until it was like some giant spider was building a com-crete and glass web a thousand stories above street level. Now, there are so many connections between the Skypillars that the sun barely pokes through – and what little does is almost lost to the permanent bed of vapor clouds near the top.

Of course, not every organization had the prestige and resources to commission their own monster building. Smaller corporations leased space in those towers. From what I'd heard, those arrangements often led to major problems between the corps. Conflicts of interest. Collusion. The kind of problems that were settled with hot steel, not lawyers.

Goons. Corpos. There was never much of a difference.

I was nearly to the Quarters' checkpoint when something caught my eye among all the skyscrapers, spotlights, and holos. Something very out of place. It stopped me dead in my tracks, and I stood, squinting into the distance.

It might have been a new ad holo projecting straight into the sky. But no, it couldn't be that...it was just too big. Too clearly defined.

It was a twisted column of flowing green light rising straight out of the middle of the city and ending somewhere in the cloud ceiling of the overcity. It was as big as a Skypillar, but it wasn't a building, and it pulsed with energy, like some sort of living thing.

I hurried over to the HMPD checkpoint on the border to Palace Park and asked the first badge I ran into if he saw the big, new, green holo. Nope, he said. I pointed right at it and asked again. Nope.

That was probably enough weird questions if I wanted to get through the checkpoint without unwanted attention, so I dropped it. I would just have to add the sighting to my growing folder of question marks. After scanning my hand and passing through the checkpoint, I focused on finding help.

I ran through my options while walking through the artificial park at the district's center, careful not to linger too long in any one place. The park was open to the public, but loitering wasn't encouraged, and there were a lot of badges on foot patrol protecting the district's higher-status residents. Even though I was trying to focus on the task at hand, I kept catching my gaze drifting over to the massive green column in the middle of the city.

From my short list of friends that might still talk to me, I landed on Alice. She was a good one from my old block. Never too snobby, and usually stuck up for me if anyone gave me crap. We were on good terms until we graduated primary, and I went off to the Quarters. The thought of hitting her up out of nowhere made me a little queasy, but I didn't have a banquet of choices in front of me.

Actually, I had *two* choices. Either com Alice outright or check her records, find her address, and knock on her door. I decided to go with the latter. For old-time's sake. And because I couldn't risk her saying no to a visit.

I hustled to the Palace Park metro station and sat on one of the dark benches near a busted overhead light. I figured it would be a good idea to stick to the shadows while I fired up my neurocom for the search, so I tucked my long hair into the collar of my sweater and pulled the hood up.

Then it was just a little matter of doing a few public searches for Alice's contact info. And when those didn't tell me anything, it was just a less than little matter of cracking into a few consumer databases until I found a drone delivery address tied to some of her food orders. It was a level of hacking that my neurocom could handle thanks to a few custom software upgrades I'd picked up working for the Luckies.

"Whoa," I whispered after reading through some of her recent deliveries. "Fresh vegetables?"

Someone had been climbing the socioeconomic ladder. The reveal made me a little nervous that she wouldn't want to see me, what with status being as important as food or oxygen in Hope.

Nah, Alice was never like that. It would be fine. Right?

"Just get the address and let's oscar," I whispered to myself.

I gathered myself back into singular focus and boarded the train leaving to the southern part of the Downtown district. Amazingly, I found a half-full car with plenty of empty seats.

Alice was living – *quartered* to be accurate – in one of the massive High-Efficiency Mixed-Allocation buildings in the Downtown area. Hers was owned by TaoCom Global – making it likely that *Alice* was also owned by TaoCom Global.

Well, well. Maybe I hadn't been the only bad decision-maker from my block.

At least TaoCom had no reason to be after me. I'd be skitz-out-of-luck if Alice landed a job at Overwatch after graduation. Since I could only assume *they* were looking for me, they'd peg me before I got into the building.

The metro wasn't known for comfort, but I needed to fix Bugger at some point. The poor guy put his life on the line – and the fact that it was my brain impulses that made him do it just made me feel that much worse about his state.

I pulled the drone from my backpack, and a few precision tools that I kept in the side pocket. Working around random bumps in the track, I mended a few severed wires and used a soldering pen to reattach his broken wing by melting the carbon fiber pivots back into place – a temporary fix, but a useful one I'd learned from my father.

A quick diagnostic with my pocket 'facer ensured that Bugger was operational, if not in the best physical shape. I returned him, along with the tools, to my backpack and slouched in my seat for the rest of the journey.

Ten minutes later, I got off the train and walked six blocks to Quadreca, the neighborhood of Downtown South dominated by HEMA-7, Alice's massive building, and a 100-story monument to modern naming conventions. 'High-Efficiency' really meant cramming as many people as possible into the building; 'Mixed-Allocation' referred to the various unit-type zones within the building itself. Commercial, residential, fabrication, labs. Probably a bit of everything.

It was a short walk through the typical light drizzle from the metro station to the building. The light rain was no deterrent in Hope Mega, and the streets were buzzing with the middle ground of the megacity's social structure. I only spotted a few corpo suits, and only a handful of homeless sleeping in the shadows out of the rain. The rest were 'the common people', wearing mostly recycled threads, mid-range cybernetics, and trying their hardest to ride the center of the trendiness bell curve.

That made it a shoulder-to-shoulder sea of wild hair in neon colors, and quite a few peeps shining the highly-fashionable stealthcore makeup look – contrasting geometric shapes and dots to confuse facial recognition software. The trend had kicked off a few years ago as a bit of fashion subterfuge against cops and corps. Then it exploded because it just looked sick.

I never tried it. I'd never even owned makeup.

By the time I made it to one of the four main entrances of Allie's building, I was already counting the levels of stores, restaurants, and offices that formed the base of the building. Twelve of them. Then there were probably 3000 residential units stacked on top of that – maybe more. Of course, HEMAs weren't nearly as tall as the Skypillars or as modern and eco-friendly as the arcologies that Hanska developed later, but they were pretty much self-contained, vertical cities in themselves.

A delivery drone buzzed over my head and then shot straight upward toward one of the building's upper floors. My eyes followed it until it became an unseeable dot among a handful of above-road vehicles floating between street level and the perpetual cloud ceiling above.

Time to head in. Crossing the threshold, I was enveloped in warm light from overhead near-infrared arrays – common fixtures in the central districts as a way to supplement sunlight and take the chill off stepping out of the rain.

I made my way through the atrium full of shops and stalls and boarded one of the lifts – then I remembered that I couldn't access her floor without a resident ID. Thankfully, HEMA-7 was old, which meant it was still using fairly bare-bones security protocols.

Plugging my 'facer into the lift controls and running one of my oh-so-useful pirated apps solved that problem in about ninety seconds.

Chapter Seven

THE OLD FRIEND

I t was a quick ride to the 28th floor. The hallway I stepped into was decorated in a Chinese aesthetic – heavy on red and gold – and I counted no less than three framed TaoCom motivational posters between the lift and Alice's door.

"This should be interesting," I muttered, pressing the call button on her access panel.

A moment later, her voice came back through the speaker.

"Yeah?"

"Hey, Allie," I said, fumbling a bit for words. "It's Jack. From Greenwood. Ya know...we were friends for like fifteen years."

A long pause.

"Jack? As in 'Jacqueline'?" the crackling voice interrupted. "What the hell? Hold on..."

I suddenly realized that I was still all tucked into my hoodie and pulled my hair back out over my shoulders before the door slid open.

Alice looked just like I remembered her. A bit shorter than me, curvier in the places you'd want to be, and wearing her deep red hair in a ponytail. The only difference worth noting was the expensive, elite-brand clothes. Stuff that kids in Greenwood couldn't even shoplift because their social rank wouldn't get them through the store entrance.

"Hey," I smiled. "Sorry for no warning."

"I do hate the pop-in," she said with a flat expression. "But I also haven't heard from you in like a year, so…"

She waved me into the apartment. That was totally her style, and it was always hard to tell if she was being sarcastically funny or genuinely perturbed.

We hugged a bit awkwardly, and then I craned my neck to take in the place Alice called home.

Her apartment was bigger than I thought it would be. From the few HEMA apartments I'd seen before, I'd figured they were all single-room units about the size of one of those storage lockers people rent to keep their car in. Hers was at least three times that size and even had a spacious bedroom and a separate cookspace in its own nook.

"Damn," I said. "This is…really nice. I'm jealous."

"Courtesy of TaoCom Global," Alice said while grabbing a couple of bottles from her fridge. "I just moved in two months ago when I made level four on the researcher track."

I flopped down on her red microfiber sofa, and she handed me one of the bottles before sitting in the matching chair opposite me. It was a New Texas lager, ice cold, featuring a big white star on the label.

"Imported beer? Look at you, drinking real beer. Eating real veggies," I said, popping the top off with an augmented finger. "Congrats on the move-up."

We clinked the bottles together and drank. The lager went down smooth and didn't have the metallic aftertaste of the Luckies' cheap, locally-engineered beers. As soon as I sat back on the sofa, a fluffy orange cat crossed the room and jumped into my lap.

"Thanks," said Alice. "And that's Jonesy. Don't pet her against the grain; she'll claw your face off. Now I have to ask...for a few reasons...what brings you to the 28th floor?"

I knew what she meant, but at least her tone wasn't outright hostile. Researchers are curious by nature, right? So she was being curious, that's all. I decided to pet Jonesy with my free hand – with the grain.

"I wanted to see you. I feel bad for not staying in touch with anyone, especially you since you always looked out for me. And in terms of coming to your door instead of comming, I just...well, I got around the lift controls. To surprise you."

Alice stared at me for a few seconds.

"Uh-huh," she said. "You know how I always told you to apply your talents toward getting somewhere better, right? I didn't mean to use them to get into *my* apartment."

Pft. Was my friend, the corpo sellout, already lecturing me on life choices?

"I'm just screwing with you," she grinned. "Please tell me that whatever you've been doing for the last year hasn't stripped you of your sense of humor. Your jokes were the only reason I liked you."

I had to laugh at that one. She still had all the weird, subversive charm of the old days.

"No, I spend most of my days laughing. Especially recently," I said.

"I can tell. Not gonna lie, Jack, you look kind of...messy. I mean, you have dead grass in your hair. Where have you been sleeping that has *grass*?"

I hadn't really thought about how much of our reunion would need to be lies. But then it dawned on me that if I wanted Alice's help, I would need to explain why, and that meant explaining pretty much everything.

I downed the rest of my beer.

"Soooo...funny story there," I began. "You know how my dad had to sign an indentureship deal with Hanska to pay off my medical bills? Then there weren't any credits coming in, just the tiny room and food allotment he got me in the contract. And I couldn't do anything about it with one arm and one leg, so I decided to get these."

"I'm guessing the funny part is how you paid for them," Alice interjected.

"Kinda. I got them from some people in the Quarters. And they let me work them off over time."

"Oh, holy skitz, Jack. Did you like, join a gang? Because if you have a record and I'm talking to you, I could lose..."

I threw up my hands and stopped her. The gesture spooked Jonesy and sent her fluffy butt running into the bedroom.

"No! No! I didn't join a gang. I was like...a freelancer paying off a debt. And I kept clean. I wasn't out breaking legs or anything, just doing tech work."

"Wow. It's gotta be hard to find an IT job in Hope's deadest and forgotten district. Didn't know homeless people needed tech support. You really lucked out."

"It's not like I was running network cable and setting up databases... Anyway, Allie, that part isn't important. It's the last job that I did. Something weird happened, and maybe you can help me figure it out."

"Uhhh, Jack...I don't know anything about ganger dynamics. I spend all my time in the Skypillar labs. I don't get out much."

I stood up, walked to Alice's fridge, pulled out two more beers, and returned to the couch. Alice took one of the bottles without comment.

"Fair enough," I continued. "I don't know if you can help, but I think I need someone to talk to. The thing is that on this last job, which was gonna be *my* last job, by the way, I ran into someone who wanted me to bring an isostick back to the Luckies. The gang. He said it would slip a tracking code and some comlogger into their neurocoms. And I did it...then they all died. I mean, I think they died."

"Oh, skitz," Alice said, sitting forward in her chair. "Like from neural shutdown darkware? Kill code stuff? That's cold...and really illegal..."

"Yeah, and what's weird is I'm pretty sure it got into my hardware, too. At the same time these guys were all...screaming...my wetgear shut down and my neurocom glitched out like crazy. Then I blacked out."

"I dunno, Jack. If it got into your system, I'm pretty sure you wouldn't be here."

"Something happened right at the same time as all of them. Not a coincidence, Allie. No way. Then I wake up and my boot tells me I have errors that weren't there before. And now I guess I'm seeing shit."

"Like glitchy AR?" Alice asked. "Like the time my cousin's NUI was rendering AR ads upside down? He got migraines every time he looked at a NuFoods poster."

"No," I chuckled, "kind of a lot bigger. After I woke up, I could see this huge, green...thing sticking up through the middle of the city."

Alice's eyebrows moved a little when I said that part, but her expression didn't change.

"What kind of green thing?"

"I don't know, Allie," I sighed and threw up my hands. "It's like a tall, skinny, swirly thing with long strings coming off it and leading, like, all over the place. But I only saw it from far off, so I don't know. I really don't."

"Jack, don't screw with me here. Does it look like…"

She made a quick swirling gesture with her finger, then rolled her eyes in frustration.

Before I could add anything, she grabbed a slate and scribbled out a string of winding lines with streaks sprouting outward along its length.

"Holy crap," I said. "That's it! So you can see it, too, and my neuros aren't busted…"

Alice jumped out of her chair and paced across the room.

"No, Jack. I can't see it. No one is supposed to be able to see it. I mean, I'm a junior tech researcher, so I *know* about it, but…no, you're really not supposed to know about this."

"Know about what? Calm down, Allie…you really lost me…"

"We can't keep talking about this. It's the highest security level. We're not talking about the kind of thing where I get laid off. More like TaoCom sends me to prison for treason and espionage."

I stood up and put my hand on Alice's shoulder.

"It's okay," I said. "And you're probably about to tell me I have to leave, and I get it. But you know something, and maybe you can just point me somewhere else I can get help. Someone who won't get fired or sent to prison, maybe?"

"I don't know, Jack. The only people who can tell you more are corporate employees. Ones much higher up than me. Even the DarkNet community doesn't know much about it because of the security level…wait!"

Alice ran to her desk terminal and scrolled through a screen of inMail messages.

"Okay, I'm doing this because I'm worried you won't be safe as long as you can see this thing. And listen, this is all I can do and you did *not* hear this from me," Alice said.

That time, her expression actually did give something away. I could see a touch of fear in the way she squinted her eyes.

She pointed to her terminal screen. "This security alert was pushed out to the entire corp last month. It talks about a 'severe threat to our most valuable network asset' and specifically a Tao-Com signal relay that was breached in the Promenade. They don't come right out and say it, but a few of us figured they were talking about...the thing *you're* talking about."

"Promenade? Yeah, I mean, it does look like the big green thing is in that direction. But I don't know how to run with that info."

"Here, at the end. There's an Overwatch report saying that they've linked the breach to a hacker...a psycher, actually. Named Zoroaster."

Psychers. Hackers that could plug their brains directly into the DarkNet. Way beyond my pay grade.

"Jack," she continued. "I've seen this guy's name come up a lot. He's dangerous. He's...killed a lot of people."

"People or corpo-rats?" I said, raising an eyebrow.

Allie frowned. I had to remember that she identified as one of them now.

"People sent to stop him from wreaking havoc," she said. "Police, Overwatch, our own security teams. He's a *terrorist*."

"I don't have much of a choice, Allie."

She stared at me a moment, then sighed. "Well, if anyone outside of TaoCom knows what happened to you, it would probably be him. Maybe he can help you fix whatever is going on up there in your hardware."

I nodded and reached for my beer, finishing it in one long swig. "Okay. So I just have to find the most wanted psycher in the mega. And, to be clear, you are going to make me *leave*? Because I came here hoping you'd let me lay low here for a while..."

Allie threw her head back and moaned. "Jack...how did it get this bad? You were easily the smartest kid in our level. A total ace with tech. I remember when you fixed that drone I found tossed out in the garbage..."

"...and when you brought over your quick cooker all panicked because you broke it," I grinned. "I fixed that, and your parents never even realized."

I thought that memory would make her smile but clearly miscalculated.

"I'm really sorry," she said, "but I can't be around you until you get that whole mess in your head figured out."

I dropped my eyes. She was right. I shouldn't drag her into my mess.

We hugged, and I thanked her for everything she'd told me. It wasn't much intel to go on, but at least I knew I was a huge walking security risk for TaoCom. And there was a chance the corpos themselves didn't actually know about me – I mean there wasn't a security alert about little ol' Jack on Alice's terminal, right? Right.

Unless Alice goes and tells them...

Nope. I kicked the thought out of my head as soon as it crept in. Things were bad enough without adding paranoia to my list of issues.

A TASTY NUBURRITO

After heading back down to street level, I figured I'd better grab something to eat. The massive HEMA building's atrium would have plenty of choices, so I strolled through the cramped shops and makeshift vendor stalls.

The atrium was like a three-story indoor reproduction of the numerous street markets in Hope Megacity. There was no shortage of bright signs, holo advertisements, and hawking retailers trying to turn an endlessly flowing crowd of shoulder-to-shoulder passersby into customers. This HEMA was considerably cleaner than the others I'd visited over the years, but somehow I expected a building that housed TaoCom employees to be even more well-kept. It was still dirty, and there were just as many out-of-service vending machines and burned out lights as anywhere else in the city.

But I suppose there's only so much you can do when your maze of print-and-assemble hallways and storefronts gets daily foot traffic in the high thousands.

I could smell a variety of different foods cooking from the minute I stepped off the lift, but nothing caught my eye right away. There was a small shop selling sushi – no doubt made from lab-grown fish substitute considering the prices; a man with a full cyber torso selling yakitori from a push cart; another shop that only sold blended drinks called 'Slurries' which had suspiciously vague ingredient lists.

Surprisingly, I hadn't seen anyone cooking a feral cat on a spit, which meant that the typical consumer in HEMA-7 was a slightly more discerning diner than those of the poorer areas. I'm sure Alice and Jonesy appreciated that fact.

After another twenty minutes of walking through the atrium, I finally settled on a NuBurrito from a tiny automat cafe in the far back corner. It was probably the most common food in Hope – the flagship product of the NuFoods Corporation was available in diners, by drone, or in vending machines – and there was something comforting about the familiarity.

I took a seat at a round metal table and bit into the wrapped mass of textured protein and lab-grown veggies. The flavor of chiles and cilantro was strong enough to mask most of the artificial aftertaste.

Absently chewing and swallowing, I thought about my next steps. How would I find an elite hacker that even Overwatch couldn't track down? I wasn't exactly part of the DarkNet underground or anything. I didn't even have any high-grade hacker connections to tap.

I had one option. Knowing there was no way in hell I was going to find this Zoroaster person, I'd have to make them come to me. That meant I needed to lure them in.

Alice said my newfound ability to see the big green column was a big deal security issue, so that had to be my best shot. I'd just need to clue Zoroaster in on it without broadcasting the info to the entire world.

Didn't need to make an enemy out of TaoCom on top of everything else.

I downed the last bite of my NuBurrito and tossed the wrapper on the ground. By the time I finished my pit stop at the nearby toilet, I'd put together a plan. Really, it was more of a loose string of half-assed ideas, but it was a place to start.

I walked back to the metro station, hoodie up, hair tucked, and head down. I needed to make my way over to the Corporate Promenade, the site of Zoroaster's breach and the apparent ground-zero of the weird green thing. Maybe if I could understand what the hell it was, I could figure out how to use it.

If not, I had a Plan B. But it really sucked compared to Plan A, so I kept my fingers crossed on the stop-and-go metro ride over to the Promenade. The metro car didn't have an active news monitor, so I watched ads flash by on the overhead panels instead.

Greysen Security was hiring. That corporation grew out of the 21st century's biggest private military contractor and now sent people all over the world to die. They also held the exclusive contract for providing Hope Mega's police force. They were always hiring.

BioDyne partnered with Severe, the trendy clothing label, to make limited-edition branded wetgear. For only half a million credits, you too could own a candy-red version of their top-shelf arm replacements, complete with a huge "Severe" logo in blocky white letters.

Ugh. I just knew somewhere, somebody was drooling themselves into a frenzy at the thought of buying those.

Then an ad from the biggest corporation in Hope Mega, High-Castle Enterprises, offering million-credit sign-on bonuses for executives with clean records who defect from other corps.

Betraying a corp sounded like a good way to die in an "accident", but greed is greed. You can't buy shiny red arms with good intentions and a winning personality.

The metro's next stop was the Promenade, the circle-jerking ground of the corporations. It had to be the most polished district in Hope, but was also the smallest at around ten square blocks. Corporate Promenade had one purpose – to peacock the hell out of the corpo lifestyle and recruit Hope denizens into the rank and file of corporate-sponsored citizenship.

Needless to say, I'd never actually been there. Although that could be said about most of the mega, not just because I spent eighteen years in the same building, but because the city itself was so huge. And of all the places I'd hope to see someday, the Promenade was not on that list.

A few overhead chimes broke my reverie and the metro doors slid open. Like it or not, this was my stop.

Chapter Nine

THE PROMENADE

I left the metro station ready to push my way through crowds of suits and eager young corpo wannabes, but there were very few people walking around. The spacious, circular plaza that made up the district's centerpiece was relatively empty except for its collection of pretentious gold statues and shimmering holograms.

They actually looked breathtaking in the misty rain falling from HighHold.

I hadn't admired them long before the glowing green column caught my eye. The flowing twist of pulsing energy looked every bit like a hologram, but it didn't give off actual light – if it were, everything around me would be washed in green. It's like it was there, but not there.

I could tell from this distance that it was about fifty feet wide across the base, and it climbed up as high as the artificial clouds that separated Hope Megacity from the overcity.

Before, from miles away, I had to squint to see the wispy strings coming off the sides, but now I could see them clearly running off in different directions, like the roots of a weed when you yank it out of a cracked sidewalk.

It was a real sight, and it was even stranger in the middle of so much stillness. I'd never seen so little action anywhere in the mega, even at two in the morning. It was so quiet I could *hear* the rain. That was a first.

My guess was that Corpo Promenade didn't have anything to offer once the recruitment offices closed for the day. And people who were hoping to land an entry-level job with a Global Corporation probably weren't out in the middle of the night.

So that left me with a little itch of worry that even being in the district this late would be suspicious. I needed to get closer to the column, but without drawing too much attention.

Sneaking was a no-go. There weren't many shadows to lurk in since the plaza was still lit up, both by huge spotlights firing straight up from the com-crete pavement and portable stand lights set up at various intervals by the HMPD. There would also be patrols, no doubt. I could dodge those, but police drones would be more difficult to avoid if they did a flyover.

For better or worse, the Promenade had been deemed a Civil Rights Exclusion Zone. Protests and "antisocial activities" were shoot-on-sight in CRE zones. Since even the roughest ganger tended to steer clear of a guaranteed bullet to the head, the badges might be a little more relaxed. Unless they *wanted* to shoot someone.

Nah. It's all good.

I stepped off toward the big green column and wound my way through the heavy-handed attempts at artistry. Between the statues, topiaries jutting from large com-crete boxes, and artful holograms dancing above the walkways, it was meant to be more like a museum than a public square.

A museum devoid of emotion or meaning, I guess.

Each step closer to the column brought it more into focus. I could see the individual green particles flowing through the intermingled tubes like sparkling dust, and the entire thing seemed to hum with vibrations I could feel in my jaw.

Once I got close enough, I saw that the column rose up from a huge, sculpted metal seal embedded in the com-crete. Like a fifty-foot-wide gold coin, it bore the image of a human heart and brain held in two winged hands – the emblem of the Consortium of Hope.

The Consortium. The ruling body of Hope Megacity, made up of capitalist giants from every corporation with a big enough stake in its development. They wrote the laws, they made the decisions, and they did it all from the clouded supercity a mile above our heads.

My eyes caught movement, and I turned to see a trio of flashlight beams bobbing in my direction. Reflective letters on the approaching shadows spelled out 'HMPD'.

Skitz.

"Hey," one of them called out. "Don't move."

All three closed the distance and circled me. They were decked out in charcoal-gray tactical gear, full armor and helmets, which made me question my optimism about them being more relaxed. The submachine guns slung across their chests didn't help.

The badge in front of me flipped up her helmet visor, shining her flashlight directly in my face. My NUI automatically kicked on a visual filter to cut back the glare, but it was still impossible to make out her features.

"Random search," she said. "What are you doing in the Promenade this evening?"

"Just looking around, ma'am," I said. "I really like the artsy holos, and we don't have trees in my district. I have to come late because I work nights. Dishwasher."

A whirring noise cut over my head as a disc-shaped PD drone joined the party. It stopped and hovered a few feet behind the lady cop, all lit up with sensors and cameras.

"Uh-huh," she said. "Have any weapons I should know about?"

Carrying was not only legal but encouraged in Hope, unless you had a violent record. I was still glad I didn't have a gun on me at that moment.

"I have a knife. It's on my belt."

The cop reached forward and lifted my hoodie, revealing the sheathed multi-knife.

"SevenArms," she said. "Good choice. Let's see your palm."

A weird request. I knew she wanted to scan my ID chip, but with the wireless tech HMPD used, they only asked to scan chips at checkpoints. She waved an RF reader across my hand and glanced over the results.

"Jacqueline Fletcher," she said, reading from the reader's screen. "You know your neurocom isn't pinging?"

I raised an eyebrow. More damage from Goodwin's code, probably.

"No," I said, trying to look innocent. "I had some errors in my NUI this morning. Thought it was a bad update."

The officer nodded. "I figured. You don't look like an opt-out."

Meaning someone who deliberately deactivated their neurocom. Doing so was a fairly aggressive middle-finger to society.

"*Dios,*" she added, still looking at the the RF reader. "*Your academic rating is up there. You should think about going into one of the recruiting offices instead of standing here looking at bushes. You don't wanna wash dishes for the rest of your life, do you?"

"No, ma'am. And…yeah, maybe I'll do that."

Not a fragging chance.

"Try GreySec. We can always use more people who appreciate good hardware," she said, gesturing at my knife. "All the better if they're not complete fragwits."

The cop waved her hand, and her two buddies walked back the way they'd come. Before falling in behind them, she leaned close enough that I could make out brown hair tucked into her helmet, full lips, and angular features that made her look something like a bird of prey.

"I know how much those things cost," she whispered, "and you don't get that kind of scrip washing dishes. Stay out of trouble, and get your neurocom patched. Alright?"

I nodded as she walked away with the whirring drone shortly behind her. Hell, if only I still had the option of staying out of trouble. Wouldn't that be something?

Once the departing flashlight beams were far enough away, I went back to examining the green column. Too bad there wasn't much else to figure out from looking at it.

I thought about the wispy strings leading away from the main column and decided to figure out where they led. That had to tell me *something*.

I picked one that coiled off away from the direction of the patrol and followed it. The strand pulsed and glowed just like the main column but about ten feet above my head. It led me to the TaoCom recruitment building.

"That can't be a coincidence," I whispered when my eyes landed on the termination point of the strand.

It ended right at a series of comm dishes and cables mounted to the side of the building about three stories up. It looked like TaoCom's signal relay, meaning it was likely the one from Alice's security report.

If Zoroaster had been in that network, there was a chance he'd still be watching it.

A good a place as any to leave a few breadcrumbs.

The bad news was that I didn't have the implants or tech to hack the relay from a distance, so I'd need to use my handheld 'facer, and that meant getting right up next to the relay.

No doubt climbing a corpo building would fall under that pesky "shoot on sight" directive, so that was out. Or at least it would have to be a very sketchy backup plan. I'd have to try reaching it with my drone first.

I switched on my pocket 'facer and attached it to the top of Bugger with a strip of speed tape from my bag, making sure the magnetic MultiWire connector was facing forward. Connecting to Bugger via my neurocom, the POV window popped up in my field of view.

"This is a bobo build," I whispered, "but I believe in you, Bugger."

Following my mental commands, Bugger climbed toward the comm relay, albeit slowly. The 'facer added weight and screwed with the drone's balance, but I managed to compensate and get him close enough to see the relay's access panel.

Of course it was closed.

"Well, this worked before," I muttered. "Take two."

I clenched my teeth and rammed Bugger into the panel. A dull 'thunk' rang out above me, but it wasn't *too* loud. Unfortunately, I had to thunk it two more times before the panel popped open.

A few deft maneuvers later, the 'facer's magnetic connector was locked onto the relay's diagnostic port. That left me juggling two wireless connections in my field of vision – Bugger's flight controls and the 'facer's data readout.

"Okay, Jack, now you're pretty much blind. Let's go, go, go." I mumbled.

It took me a few minutes – long, anxious minutes – but I managed to find a pretty mundane data stream passing through the relay. It repeated in cycles, maybe a beacon or identifier. Not really the type of tech I was used to, so I took a guess and planted a few extra bits of data.

Hopefully, the corpos would ignore it, but this Zoroaster person would take the time to figure it out. And the psycher would be able to contact me once they realized that I planted a coded version of my neurocom ID — every digit multiplied by a successive prime number. It was the best I could think of on the spot, and legendary super-hackers are supposed to be good with math.

I just hoped it didn't chime with TaoCom.

"That should do it," I sighed, guiding Bugger back down into my outstretched palm. "Fingers crossed."

A few minutes later, I had my drone and 'facer stowed, and was walking back toward the metro.

I didn't even make it onto the train before my NUI chimed a notification for an unknown caller. I stopped, nursed a split second of hesitation, then boarded the train and accepted the com.

Chapter Ten

THE RETRO CAFE

"Hello?" I thought, grabbing a handhold as the metro lurched into motion.

"This is NCID 62236-2141, right?"

It was a younger guy's voice. Better than someone from Overwatch immediately telling me to put my hands up and report to the nearest prison, but I was still shaking.

"Yeah, it is," I replied.

"What do you want?"

"I need to talk to Zoroaster. I can see a weird column of light in the Promenade, and someone told me he can help."

A stretch of uncomfortable silence.

"Café 2020, one hour," the guy said. "Come alone, and tell the hostess you're meeting Erik Mander. Got that?"

"Uhm, okay. What's a 'hostess'?" I asked.

"Do *not* accept any other comms. Your ID is compromised," he replied.

The call ended. Unregistered neurocoms weren't exactly common – or legal – so there was a good chance it was Zoroaster. An equal chance it could have been Overwatch or some other corporation. Either way, they worked fast, and I had no options.

I plotted a course for Café 2020, and the MegaMaps app gave me a forty-eight-minute ETA.

"Weird," I mumbled. "Downtown North. It's right next to the NiceSlice."

I spent the rest of the metro ride thinking about Alice and one of the first long trips she'd ever convinced me to go on when we were kids. A harmless meetup at a pizza shop. Except that it wasn't. Kids aren't known for their delicate handling of people who are different.

And that day, they figured out I was *really* different.

A short metro ride later, I plodded through puddles at street level, closing in on Café 2020. This part of Downtown North was a brightly-lit collection of restaurants, shops, and low-rent hotels meant for tourists. Foot traffic was a complete one-eighty from the Promenade, and groups of laughing consumers streamed in and out of the various establishments.

I figured blending would be easy enough, but the crowds made it near impossible to tell if anyone was following me. Out of the corner of my eye, I spotted the neon signage of the NiceSlice pizza joint, the site of a long-repressed teenage trauma that was better off buried.

"Ugh," I muttered, averting my eyes.

No matter. The Café 2020 was just ahead, glowing with all of its retro-themed gaudiness.

The restaurant stood apart from the typical aesthetic of Hope Mega, being one of the only establishments I've ever seen with large panel windows looking in. Rather than rows of digital signs, key spots in the windows held legacy paper posters with labeled illustrations of classic food: baked potato, meatballs on noodles, and something called a "cheesesteak".

I dodged through a crowd of exiting patrons, entered the café, and scanned the large dining room for anyone who looked suspicious. The place was crowded, loud, and heavily decorated with relics from the early 21st century.

"Table for one, *my guy*?" a voice came from behind.

I turned, and a teenage girl in short shorts and a weird smock smiled at me. The café's logo on the smock told me she worked here.

"Uh, are you the...hostess?"

"That's what they call me, *fam*," she said, still smiling.

Did this girl get hit in the head or something? What the hell is a *fam*?

"Okay," I said, one eyebrow raised. "then I'm here to meet Erik Mander."

The girl's eyes twitched so fast I almost didn't catch the movement. Then she waved me into the dining room.

I followed her through rows of round tables packed with people chowing on hamburgers, meatballs, and a dozen other things I couldn't identify from the posters.

"Is the food here...real?" I asked the hostess.

"Printed to order, but based on authentic twenty-first-century recipes and images," she answered without turning around.

We walked through the dining area and into a back corridor, the walls covered in old technology. There was a display of little flat devices that looked kind of like my palm 'facer labeled 'Smart Phones', and something that looked like a huge version labeled a 'Smart TV'.

I remembered my history modules well enough to think that calling anything from that time 'smart' was a bit of a stretch.

"Sooo...where are we going?" I asked as we turned a corner and passed the bathrooms.

"To Erik Mansen," she said, the bubbliness gone from her voice.

"You mean Erik *Mander*, right?"

"Whatever. I'm not a fragging super-spy or anything. I'm just doing this because your boyfriend gave me a hundred scrip."

She stopped at the door marked 'FIRE EXIT'.

"And 'cuz he's hot," she added, pushing open the door with a cutting grin.

I took the cue and exited into the back alley. A few overhead lights flickered, buzzing with flies drawn to the piles of trash bags all around. The smell of rotting food was overpowering.

"Thanks," I said, nose fully wrinkled.

"Have fun with your little secret hookup or whatever," the hostess said, slamming the door and trapping me outside with the smell.

Stuck outside in the stinking darkness, a sudden flash of anxiety swept over me. If some corpo was planning to black bag me or zero me with a sniper rifle, I probably just fell right into his perfect little trap.

This is *not* how I would have set up a meeting. Damn, I hate being stuck with no options.

"Jacqueline?" a half-whisper came from somewhere above me.

I couldn't see anything but tall com-crete walls and flickering shadows. "Yeah, I'm Jack."

Faster than I could flinch, a guy dropped from above and landed right in front of me. The sudden entrance wasn't even the most off-putting part. Most of his body was a mirage of shifting colors that matched the backdrop, making him almost invisible. It looked like the head of a clean-cut Asian guy in his twenties was hovering in front of me.

"What the complete fu…" I started, but the words drowned in fear-adrenaline before they could escape.

"Chill," the guy said, and now I recognized the voice from the unknown com. "It's a rep suit, man. Active camo. I gotta take you to Z. Do you trace?"

It was a lot to take in at once. Active camo suit, explains the floating head. Got it. Take me to Z. Must mean Zoroaster. Got it. That left…

"Trace?"

The guy rolled his eyes. "Trace! Run, jump, slide, rooftops, walls…"

"Oh, like a runner! Like a *runner* runner," I said, "No. Not even a little."

"Then climb on. Can't hang around here. We need to oscar," he said, turning around and crouching.

This would be interesting. Runners were another cottage industry of the mega, hired for their acrobatic climbing and jumping skills, making them expert urban navigators. I'd heard of runners carrying data, drugs, or just working surveillance, but never of them giving piggy-back rides.

"I'm fully-limbed, man," he said, probably sensing my apprehension. "I can handle the weight. Let's go."

Yet again, what choice did I have? I climbed aboard and held on like my life depended on it.

"You let go, you splat," he said, confirming that my life did indeed depend on it. The guy nodded once, then darted up the wall.

The speed that he climbed made my guts want to fall out. He wasn't just fully limbed — cybernetic arms and legs — he had to be rocking suction grips or something. Strength alone can't make someone climb the side of a building like an insect.

We hit the top about thirty stories up, and he flung us both onto the rooftop with one arm. That's when curiosity and mild anxiety became terror. The guy stepped to the edge of the building, clearly intent on leaping across a four-lane street to a building on the next block.

"I'm so gonna pee on your expensive chameleon suit," I groaned.

I thought I heard him chuckle, but didn't have time to process it before his feet left the rooftop. For what seemed like an eternity, there was nothing but wet, rainy wind, streaming lights, and the sound of my heartbeat pumping in my ears.

The runner's arms and legs hissed when we hit the next building, some kind of shock absorbers that let him stick to the wall without bouncing off. He was clearly built for this job.

"Higher now," he said. "Away from street-level cameras and eyeballs."

Another twenty stories up and we were on a new rooftop, this one high enough that I could see over some of the surrounding buildings. If not for the terror stabbing needles into my brain, it would have been a nice view – bits of Hope skyline lit up in the night, dancing holograms, and those paper lanterns that show up everywhere.

I didn't have long to enjoy it anyway. The guy went full-on trace mode and took the next three rooftops like he was jumping over puddles. Again and again, I felt the rush of wind as we flew, then the crunch of impact onto the top of a building.

Wind, crunch. Wind, crunch. My organic arm and leg were starting to get sore from holding on and shaking at the same time. Finally, he came to a stop at the edge of a roof overlooking a dark parking structure. It was painfully far away and at least twenty stories down.

"Big finish," the runner said, then took the farthest leap yet.

I closed my eyes. The wind was rushing by for *way* too long this time...

Crunch. Hey, I was still alive. He'd nailed the landing.

"Hop off."

I opened my eyes and dropped to my feet, both shaking so badly I wasn't sure if even cybernetics could keep me standing. We'd made it to the top of the parking structure, alone and surrounded by dormant cars and late-night shadows.

"That's you," the runner said, pointing toward a black transport van with its side door open.

Then he turned and leaped into the night, disappearing before I could even guess where he was planning to land.

A horrifying trip, and now I had a shady van to look forward to.

As soon as I got near the open door, two sets of gloved hands reached out and pulled me inside. I struggled purely out of instinct, but it was pointless. One of them quickly pinned me against a seat with the kind of gorilla strength that only came from high-end wetgear arms; the other grabbed my backpack and rifled through it before tossing it on the floor behind them.

The door slid shut and locked as they worked. Both of my captors – escorts? – wore hoodies and half masks, so I couldn't make them out. I could only tell that the one who searched my bag was a girl when she started talking.

"Hold still," she said, her eyes flashing blue as she stared into my face.

She must have been scanning me. Verifying my identity, I guess.

"Alright, now I've got to put this on you," she said, pulling a weird-looking beanie cap off the van's floor.

The hat looked like it was made of a reflective material and had a web of wires running around the outside. When she pulled it over my head, my NUI flashed a notification that I'd disconnected from the network and that MiFi was out of range.

"Alright," the girl called out. "She's OTG."

Off the grid. The hat was some kind of neurocom jammer.

Gorilla-arms released their ape grip, and the van zoomed forward with an electric purr.

"You'll have to keep that on until we get where we're going," the masked girl continued. "Don't mess with it."

"Uhm...okay," I said.

"Don't take it personally; we've just got a lot of security protocols. Z runs a tight ship, but that's why we're all still kicking."

I thought about asking questions — or even just saying something to break the silence — but all I could think up was idle chatter that seemed pretty out of place for a shadowy van abduction, so I kept shut.

The van had no windows or outside monitors, so there was nothing to see from inside the cargo area. Other than two rows of seats facing each other, it was pretty much stripped bare. The only piece of hardware I noticed was a portable 3D printer about the size of a shoebox.

By the time the van rolled to its final stop, I figured we must have driven half the length of the city. Gorilla-arms opened the door, and my masked companions jumped out and stood outside the door for me to follow. I slid out of the van into a dimly-lit indoor space.

Once my eyes adjusted, I saw we'd parked inside a garage with enough room for three or four more vehicles. Tools and spare parts were scattered around the bay, and there was a single red door on the back wall.

I waited for someone to lead me to the next step, but the two masks were paying more attention to a vid on a handheld slate held between them.

Eventually, the van's driver jumped out of the front seat and circled around to me. He looked to be in his twenties and had a few long scars on the shaved side of his head – the other part was covered in spiky raven-black hair. Surprisingly, he wasn't wearing a mask or hood, but he was dressed in drab colors like his companions.

"You forget the rest of your costume?" I asked.

"Nah," he grinned back and pointed at the van's windows. "Dark tint does the job. I'm Mallus."

"I'm Jack."

"I know. Name, weight, and shipping requirements are on the cargo manifest."

"There's a cargo manifest for a shady street pickup? Your guy really does love protocol." I said, raising an eyebrow.

"Nah, girl," Mallus laughed, "I'm messin' with you."

"Hey," the masked girl chimed in, looking up from the slate. "Quit flirting. Z's waiting."

Mallus made a 'whoops' gesture and waved for me to follow him. He unlocked the red door using both a coded keypad and a biometric eye scan – tight security for a junky auto shop – and we headed down a metal spiral staircase surrounded by old cement walls.

The stairs ended in a short hallway leading to a very sturdy-looking metal door. Mallus tapped a faded and peeling sign on the wall reading 'FALLOUT SHELTER'.

"Prepper bunker," he said. "Some Third War survivor probably had this custom built after they moved to the mega. Still afraid of bombs."

"Maybe they just wanted a place to hide from the corpo-rats," I said. "They're a lot worse than being nuked."

Mallus chuckled and looked at me sideways before popping the heavy latch on the door.

"You'll fit in here," he said with a broad smile. "Step in. Z's inside. Oh, and you can take off that hat now. Scope you later...gotta roll."

Mallus rattled off the words and rushed back up the stairs so fast I barely caught all of it.

"So long," I said, but he was already closing the red door behind him.

Chapter Eleven

THE BUNKER

I stepped through the bulky hatchway, and the door shut behind me with a loud metallic clank. I was alone in a small room with maps and printouts covering the walls. The place looked like it was made from concrete blocks, a sure sign it was not built with permission from the Consortium.

There were a few crates in the corner marked "RATIONS: PROPERTY GREYSEC", along with a stack of legacy printed books almost as tall as the ceiling. Past all of the clutter, there was another metal door set into the far wall.

"More books than I've seen my whole life," I whispered to myself.

A quiet buzzer sounded, and the far door opened wide. The dark-skinned man that stepped through wore a brown duster over a skin-tight NetOps suit with the usual conduits and sensors. His shaved head was nearly covered with neural implants. Definitely a committed psycher.

"Jack," he said softly, sticking out his hand. "I am Zoroaster."

I shook his hand, remembering a bit too late to pull the OTG hat off my head.

"These precautions are necessary," he continued, grinning. "You're an unknown quantity right now. But if what you hinted at is true, we'll take more permanent steps to keep you off the grid."

"Oh, it's true. I just don't know what it means."

Zoroaster gestured toward the open door and smiled.

"Come in here, and I'll show you."

The adjoining room was three times as big as the first, completely lined with flashing networking equipment and cabling. A well-worn NetOps station sat in the middle, looking like a very high-tech salon chair with numerous cables and coolant tubes running to and from it.

Multiple screens were mounted to one wall, each displaying a running stream of network logs and code readouts – except for the center screen which showed a 3D map of the stacked cities, Hope on the bottom and HighHold above it.

That's the screen Zoroaster walked me to.

"Do you know how many street-level denizens of the megacity have ever made it up to HighHold?" he asked. "As far as I can tell, zero. The City of the Giants is off limits to anyone who wasn't born into the most elite corpo families."

"What about the corpos with citizenship? And the ones who make it up the ranks and become execs? Isn't the whole sales pitch that you can work your way up the tower until you're living above the clouds?"

"Motivational half-truth to keep everyone productive. The Consortium didn't name this place Hope out of a sense of irony. They named it after the biggest resource they wanted to mine out of it. Driven, loyal, and tireless labor based on rabid aspiration."

"Nothing new about another corpo lie. I assume everything coming from above is straight BS."

"And you should. After the war, TaoCom monopolized data infrastructure and created the first neurocom network. Now they own MediaOne and all the ad production throughout the Mega. I've been paying special attention to their corporation for a few years, ever since they got into a cold war with HighCastle. And I think what you've discovered has something to do with that rivalry."

"TaoCom taking on HCE? How is that a good idea?" I asked.

"Everyone assumes HighCastle is the undisputed god among corporations. At least in this part of the world," said Zoroaster, "but it's a lot more complex than that. They have a monopoly on space exploration and rare resources and that makes them powerful, but they rely on other corps to stay running. They especially depend on TaoCom's net tech and orbital telecom infrastructure, which gives HighCastle the mad itch for 'vertical integration'."

"Meaning what?"

"Meaning HighCastle thinks space is *their* show. Some of their execs think they should just take over the satellites, control the network themselves. That cuts out a lot of costs and hassle on their part and actually makes some sense, which is why the question that's been eating away at me for years is not 'why would they?' but 'why haven't they?'."

"The war in Europa? TaoCom is Chinese, and BlueCastle is New Euro Union, already killing each other for years. Pour gas on that fire, and someone might forget about Hope Mega's...what's it called..."

"Sovereignty," Zoroaster added. "I don't think that's it. The whole reason the most powerful people in the world decided to share one city is to have insurance against that sort of thing. You won't get nuked by the family that lives one building over."

"So even the corpos realized they would end up killing each other to extinction if they didn't...what...let themselves and their own families be held hostage? Nice."

"It's worked for the last seventy years or so," Zoroaster grinned. "They're smart. Very smart in everything they do. That's how they built HighHold, and that's how they remain in the seat of power up there without question."

"Alright, a fun history lesson. But where does my broken NUI fit into any of this?"

"Your interface is not broken," Zoroaster waved off the notion. "Listen, there's more I want you to know so you can understand what's happened to you. So, the reason HighCastle continues to stand down is that TaoCom owns something too important to risk. It took me years of scraping and listening to figure out what that could be, but three months ago I cracked a system in the Promenade district and got my first real clue.

"All it was, was a glimpse. Massive amounts of network traffic with zero latency, all encrypted and moving with no carrier signature. I could only pull out one repeating alphanumeric string before my parser overloaded..."

Zoroaster touched the display screen, and a series of characters popped up: 'BeanStalk'.

"What the hell is a beanstalk?" I asked.

"A *real* beanstalk? That's the plant that beans would come from before they were synthed in labs. But that's not really the important part. In this case, it's just a clue to what I'd found."

He stepped away from the screen.

"Massive amounts of data have to move between Hope and High-Hold," Zoroaster continued. "The puppeteers need to have their strings in hand. And we know that there's no physical access from below the cloudline to the overcity. Even the Skypillers have multi-level bulkheads with no doors around cloud level. That's why we've never found large trunks of cabling running from Hope to HighHold. They probably don't exist."

"So they use emwave, right? Or wireless?"

"That's not possible. We're talking real-time data generated by a hundred-million people. And drones, cameras, traffic control, and comms. Anything coming from street-level corpo buildings that needs to be securely sent up the top execs. That's more data than any system we know about can handle. Which means…"

"It's a system we *don't* know about," I added.

"That was my thought. They use legacy comms on street level, but there's some kind of newtech data stream running between the megacity and the overcity. When you told me you could see a glowing column running from the Promenade up into the clouds, it confirmed it. You saw the BeanStalk."

"So, Overwatch fried my neurocom, and now I can see data flying through the air?"

"Doubtful," Zoroaster said. "More likely, you accidentally tapped into some kind of monitoring and maintenance system. Like a visual representation of whatever this BeanStalk is. Maybe engineers use it to troubleshoot the data stream. And this would be high-level, like HighHold engineers only."

"And maybe the top rats at Overwatch, right? It was one of their kill programs that started all this."

Zoroaster nodded. "It's possible."

"That's why you jumped on the chance to get me here," I said. "You want to destroy this thing."

Zoroaster walked to the NetOps chair and leaned against it. He thought for a moment before responding.

"If you were being held hostage and your captor left a gun next to you, would you dismantle it so he no longer had a gun, or would you shoot him with it and escape?"

"So...you don't want to take it away from them. You want to use it. Against the corporations?"

"That's right, Jack. I figure the best we could hope for by destroying the BeanStalk is widespread chaos and probably some very violent corporate crackdowns. Anarchy is just a fantasy for the desperate, not a solution. What we have is a real chance at a solution."

"We're *not* desperate?"

"No," Zoroaster smiled. "We're just different. We refuse to play their game, and that means we lose by forfeit. But when that's the situation, the answer isn't to flip the board over and scatter the pieces – then the suffering just goes on. We need to cheat."

Zoroaster just let the words hang in the air while he watched my face. He was obviously a smart hombre, but that didn't mean he was right, and didn't mean I could trust him any more than I could trust a corpo. He said it himself – corpos were smart.

But I *was* being hunted. And I still had old debts to pay.

"Alright," I said finally. "Let's say I help you cheat the corpos. You have to help me get my father out of servitude."

"Hm. I'm guessing that's a lot of scrip."

"Six figures. But that's gonna have to be the deal," I said, crossing my arms.

"Then I will do the best I can with the resources I have."

"That's not good enough, Z."

"They're considerable resources, Jack," the psycher grinned.

He held that knows-too-much grin and raised his fist in front of him. I bumped it with my own.

"Deal," I said. "But I gotta know…what are *you* getting out of all this?"

Zoroaster stood back up and clapped his hands together.

"More information, Jack. The BeanStalk is a secure line right into the giants' deepest secrets. We want to find out every trick and tool they have for keeping themselves up there and us down here. Then we use those tools ourselves. We're going to look behind the curtain and see who the wizard really is."

"The curtain, huh?" Zoroaster sure had a lot of weird metaphors in his conversational grab bag. "And what do I have to do? You still haven't said that part."

He walked over to one of the racks of networking gear and pushed a button. A latching noise echoed through the room, and the entire rack of hardware slid along the wall to reveal another metal door.

"You rest. You look like you haven't slept in days," he said, waving me into the secret door. "There's a few more rooms back here. Bathroom, cots. A small cookspace."

I walked through the door to a short corridor with an open room on the left and two closed doors on the right. Zoroaster popped the latch on the first door and swung it open. Inside was a small living space with two cots and a metal toilet.

"You can stay in this one. No one uses this part of the shelter, not unless there's an emergency. You'll have it all to yourself. The room across the hall has a dining table and appliances – be careful not to start any fires. I have some books in there if you like to read."

I poked my head into the open room to see for myself. A box-shaped quick cooker, a hotplate, and a mini-fridge were lined up on a counter. Against the far wall was a bookshelf and…

"Is that a vending machine?" I asked, eyes widening.

"Yeah," Zoroaster chuckled. "That's one of my upgrades. Head-Rush machine, ten flavors, all free. Had to take it apart to get it down here, but it was worth it."

"Nice," I said. "But I'm more into that cot in the other room right now. Like you said…days without sleep."

"No doubt. I'm gonna close you in here for safekeeping. This place was wired with an analog intercom, so you can buzz me if you need anything. This button, right here on the wall. Once you're ready for the next step, we'll get to work."

I thanked Zoroaster, and he wished me pleasant dreams before sealing me into the extra-secret living quarters of the already secret bunker. Everything was moving fast, but I wasn't kidding about being worn down. I needed to crash out for real.

First, I opened the mini-fridge and was very happy to find a cold bottle of purified water. I chugged it down and headed for bed.

The cot was comfortable enough, especially since my last rest was when I zonked under a pile of scrap metal. It didn't take long for me to fall asleep, and when I did, I dreamed of Alice.

Chapter Twelve

THE DREAM

I found myself in the tiny apartment I shared with my dad, fully aware that I was dreaming thanks to the *LucidSleep* app – TaoShop top app download from 2159 to 2161.

My gaze immediately drifted to the metal crutch leaning against my desk, and I knew that I was seeing through the eyes of my thirteen-year-old self – after mom died, but before dad left to become a Hanska servile.

At that age, the desk and chair were my home. I spent hours studying at the terminal or learning about something new from the net. When I needed to go to the cookspace or bathroom, I used the single crutch to make the daring trek from one side of the apartment to the other.

For at least ten years of my childhood, I'd hardly left that two-room world. Dad said it would be too dangerous, and really, crutching around a crowded city with one working arm and leg was a massive hassle. So instead, I counted on a few friends to bring the world to me, and Alice had always been reliable with the outside news and friendly visits.

I closed out the remote schooling app on the terminal in front of me and closed my eyes to drink in the memory. My schoolwork for the day was done, which meant I should be getting a visit very soon...

The door chime rang through the room.

"Front door, open," I said, and the door slid wide with a soft hiss.

Alice walked in wearing her usual smile. It always seemed to enter the room a few nanoseconds before the rest of her. At first glance, she looked like the 20-year-old version of herself I'd just talked to in the waking world, but I blinked, and she became true to my memory of her younger self; stick skinny, bright pink hair and wearing the most fashionable threads she could find by scouring through recycling shops. Her favorite backpack, designed to look like a furry white cat hanging off her shoulders, was slung over one arm.

It only took her five steps to cross the small room and sit on the couch nearby. That couch was where my dad slept for a few hours every morning, since he'd always insisted I take the single bedroom. She pushed aside a pile of blankets and pillows to make a spot for her fuzzy backpack.

"Alright, Jack," she said. "I know you're glad the course module is over, right? I can't wait to get back to science and tech classes. History is so boring."

"Yeah," I said. "It's *all* kinda boring."

"You mean it's easy. There's a difference. It'll get harder once we move on to post-primary classes."

"Corpo-sponsored higher education. Sounds fun," I groaned.

"Pfft. Who cares if it's fun? It leads to job placement so you can get the scrip to pay for your own fun. I'm thinking about HighCastle if I can keep my grades up."

"Planning to move to space and leave me here?" I asked through a flat expression.

"No way! You can come with me. As long as *you* keep your grades up. The way you're going, you can have your pick of corporations."

"Yeah, Allie. The girl who can't even leave her apartment is going to leave the planet. Sign me up now."

Alice sighed and sat back on the couch.

"None of that pity crap, Jack. And if anything, being stuck here for ten years should make you want to get as far away as possible. Doesn't get much farther than an orbital platform."

I loved Alice, but I hated being reminded that the only way I'd ever escape my limitations would be by bowing to a corporate master.

"The other megacities are farther," I frowned. "Lonestar. That's pretty far. Cascadia's like 1500 miles away. Orbital platforms are only 200 miles up."

"You know what I mean," Alice chuckled. "Anyway, I need you to come with me somewhere. Tonight."

My eyes nearly popped out of my skull. Why was I dreaming about a day of being constantly triggered? Alice knew that asking me to leave the apartment was probably going to lead to an argument.

"C'mon, Allie..." I moaned.

"It's a group thing. Other kids from our remote ed track – good ones. Someone put it together through the social board. We're just going to meet at the NiceSlice in Downtown North."

"Uhm. That's like an hour on the metro, isn't it?"

"It was the most central spot. Everyone's spread out all over the mega, and we're all excited about meeting each other in person. Hey, they even *asked* me to make sure you come."

Allie smirked and punched me in the arm before adding, "They probably want to meet the girl who's making all their test scores look bad."

"I don't know," I said, turning away from her. "Things are so bad here. Dad was telling me we might have to move out of this HEMA because it's too expensive. He's still trying to pay off my medical debt and…"

"So? I'll buy your pizza. I'm not letting you off the hook over a few stupid creds."

"But it just feels wrong. He works all day, every day. Just to pay bills that he wouldn't even have if I hadn't been born…like this. How can I just go out and have fun?"

Alice stared at me for a few seconds like she was trying to solve a math problem. She was good at those, so it made me worry a bit.

"And your dad does all of this sacrificing so you can live in a box? What's the point of all that work if you never actually *do* anything? Call me crazy, but I think living a little fun would be like thanking him."

I sighed. People said 'discipline' was choosing what you should do over what you want to do. Not helpful. I didn't want to do much of anything, and I wasn't too sure about what I *should* do either.

Kids who wanted to grow up climbing the ranks in the Skypillars had it easy. The path to corpo placement was pretty clear, and once they signed up, their corporations had no problems laying out the rest of their lives.

Even people who were fine staying street level knew what they wanted, even if it was just another drink or enough scrip to hit a club every night. But I was stuck somewhere in the middle, and I didn't have any easy-to-follow guideposts.

"You're thinking about it, I can tell," Alice smiled. "Come on. I even brought you some clothes. My favorite outfits. You can't say no to that."

I threw my head back and let out a loud groan. "Fine. Let's see what you brought me."

Alice squealed and clapped before opening up her cat backpack. Then things got hazy.

A loud chime rang out in the back of my skull, followed by a soothing, feminine voice:

> *Thank you for using* LucidSleep*! This dream was sponsored by NuBurrito! Grab breakfast – then grab today by the balls!*

Chapter Thirteen

THE PUCK

I opened my eyes to the interior of the shelter and felt surprisingly refreshed. I dismissed a string of "no connection" alerts in my NUI before making use of the cold metal toilet. Next stop was the open room across the hall.

My mouth was bone dry, so I headed straight to the vending machine and hit the button for a HeadRush flavor called "Fiesta Loco" – prickly pear, jalapeno, and agave, all infused into the proprietary HeadRush blend of stimulants and grain alcohol.

It was probably safe to say that 90% of people living at street level relied on HeadRush to get through the day. The tagline on the front of the machine said it all: 'The Drink That Fuels Hope!'

My stomach wasn't growling, but I figured I'd better consume something solid. I was craving a NuBurrito, but only managed to find a box of ration gel packets while rummaging through the cupboard. Semi-solid would have to work. Each packet read '100% daily requirement vitamins, electrolytes, macronutrients'. Not bad for something the size of my hand.

I emptied one pouch into my mouth and washed it down with the HeadRush before realizing the gel was flavored like cooked salmon. It was not a good combo. A few more swigs of Fiesta Loco eliminated the unsavory finish.

It was time to get to work, whatever that actually meant. I went to the intercom console in the hall and buzzed for Zoroaster. A minute later, the hidden door clanked open, and he waved me back into the NetOps room.

"All rested up?" Zoroaster asked.

"Best sleep I've had in a while."

"Greysen Arms has their demons, but they make some good hardware. They put as much effort into designing their cots as they do their armored vehicles," Zoroaster grinned.

"So, how do we get this started?" I asked.

Zoroaster smacked his palm against the NetOps chair's padded seat.

"Jump up. First thing is scans. Going to check your wetgear and neural implant for errors. See if we can't figure out how you survived a kill code and why you can see the BeanStalk. Then I'll make some upgrades to your network firmware so you can leave the shelter and stay off the grid."

"That'll be nice. Not that I'm in any hurry. If we can get food delivered here, I might wear out my welcome."

Zoroaster chuckled while I climbed into the chair.

"You'll get sick of it eventually. Those other kids that picked you up...they've all spent time hiding out in those rooms. From corpos or cops, depending. I couldn't pay them to spend another night down here."

They must not have targets on their backs anymore, I thought, as Zoroaster pulled a few cables from the racks of tech lining the walls and walked them toward the chair.

He held the cables up and smiled. "Nothing you haven't done before. Stand by."

He plugged one cable into my neurocom's diagnostic port and another into my isostick reader. The last bit of prep was setting a neural waveform scanner on my forehead. Then Zoroaster pushed a wheeled terminal next to the chair.

"High-level scan first," he said, tapping the terminal screen. A data transfer notification popped up in my NUI.

"Alright, there are some errors here. Common stuff. I doubt they're related to the BeanStalk. I'm going to have to clear those up before I upgrade your networking."

"You sure they're not important?" I asked.

"Positive. Anything BeanStalk has to be buried way deeper than this. These are just partial updates and some corrupted engrams. Same thing a druggo would wake up with if he passed out outside of MiFi range."

"Alright. Good."

A few more taps on the terminal.

"Wait a sec..." Zoroaster mumbled. "What is this now? You have wetgear installed that's not in your medical records."

"I got the arm and leg from gangers," I said. "Not really official channels."

"Doesn't matter. As soon as your neural implant interfaced with the cybernetics, it would update your records. This is different. Deliberately blocked from syncing with the Consortium's asset management database. A CNS implant in your spine."

"Oh, the puck," I said. "I got that when I was really young. I was a 'very sick baby', and that thing pretty much kept me alive. And it's how dad got into debt."

"A 'puck', huh?" Zoroaster continued. "It looks like it's tapped into your limbic system. Hm. And your endocrine, and lymphatic. Then wired directly into your neurocom. Whatever this thing is, I'll bet you a million credits this thing is what saved you from the kill code."

That means dad saved me again, even from however far away he was serving his contract.

"Do you know who made it?" Z asked. "There are no signatures on this thing."

"TaoCom, according to my boot screens, but BioDyne sent the bill. Dad didn't talk about it much, so I really don't know much about it."

"Well, I guess we hit paydirt on day one," Zoroaster chuckled. "That's got to be why you're seeing the BeanStalk. Maybe there's similar tech in the puck, or some kind of integrated data stream that got kicked on while it was fighting off the kill code."

He tapped more controls.

"Alright, we're getting somewhere," he continued. "Let me clear these error codes and do the OTG upgrades real quick."

Zoroaster worked on that terminal for another three hours before we were finished with what he called 'our first session'. According to him, he'd masked my neurocom signatures, routed my MiFi through a botnet of proxies, and removed any trackers he'd found.

Things got way more interesting when he cranked his dive up to eleven. I knew things were getting serious when he jacked another cable from the NetOps chair into one of his own neural implants.

I'll admit, I didn't know much about psychers – hackers who interfaced directly with tech – other than that they were geared up a lot like brainers. Direct neural ports, bio- and cyber-enhanced nervous systems, that sort of thing. I knew they could stay mobile and live pretty normal lives, unlike brainers who gave up the real world to be living computers.

"With this implant, I can use my subconscious as a processor," he said, noticing my curiosity. "Over a hundred thousand calculations per millisecond – but the real benefit is that my engrams do a lot of the decryption and collating for me without having to consciously think about it."

"So that's how it works," I said. "I thought it was like the old cinemas. Like you 'take a walk through cyberspace' or something. Like the MetaNet but...better."

Z laughed.

"Do a lot of people still think that?" he was still chuckling. "No, that's just old science fiction. They had these crazy ideas about 'cyberspace' that actually ended up being more like the MetaNet we have now. Just a nice UI for navigating data, playing games, and shopping.

"The whole point of interfacing directly with a computer is to speed things up. If I had to walk around in a virtual world pushing buttons and waving data around, I might as well just use a slate."

"I never thought of that." I mumbled.

"Deep interfacing is more like dreaming. My subconscious does most of the work and serves what's important up to my conscious mind. Right now, I'm sifting through thousands of terabytes of data, but I'm not seeing one thousandth of a percent of it. I only have to deal with what my brain knows I'm looking for."

Before long, Z found something that fit that request. He uncovered a huge cache of buffered data in a hidden partition in my brain – and he suspected it was stuff I'd somehow skimmed out of the BeanStalk.

"This is great, Jack. It'll give me somewhere to start. I can get a feel for this data and figure out how to collate it. We'll be listening in on the best-kept secrets in corpo history in no time."

I'd only just met the man, but I couldn't imagine him ever looking this happy.

"Sick," I said, jumping out of the chair. "Let's hope that pays off."

"Information always pays off. Now I suggest you head topside and get some fresh air. Doctor's orders."

"I can live with that. You really a doctor?"

"I'm BioDyne trained and a former junior associate at Benchmark Medical."

"Ah," I grinned, "Benchmark. '*The Essence of Convalescence.*' No wonder you know so much about high-level corpo life."

"The very same," he chuckled. "And it's why I know so much about rigged games. Now get upstairs and try to find some sunshine. These NIR and vitamin D lamps can only do so much."

I thanked Zoroaster again and made for the exit by way of the spiral staircase one room over. Once back in the garage, I was a little surprised to see no one around. Even the van that had brought me was gone.

I made it as far as the outer door when my neurocom chimed with a letter "Z" flashing in the corner of my vision.

"Yeah," I said, answering the com.

"It's me. I tapped a relay outside the bunker to test your comms. Everything looks secure on this end, so feel free to make any calls you want. Just remember that the weakest link in the security chain is never the tech, so don't tell anyone *anything*. No one, okay?"

"You got it. I don't even know who I would tell," I said and disconnected.

Except I *did* know. I would tell Alice if she was willing to talk to me again, but I wasn't ready to knock on that door yet. She was right. Talking to me could bring heat down on her, and I didn't want to take that chance.

Chapter Fourteen

THE SHOPS

I banged the outer door of the garage open and stepped into a welcome breeze. Looking up to check my bearings, I saw that I was just below the very northern edge of the HighHold clouds. Being so far at the edge of the Mega, there was a good amount of sun on my face. It felt a hell of a lot nicer than the Near-Infrared lamps in the bunker.

Growing up, one of those lamps had been my best friend. Getting real sunlight when you live in the shadow of an overcity is hard enough, but it was even harder when I never left my apartment.

No, not *never*. There were a few times early on. I tried scrounging around alleys for old tech, and of course the awful outing to NiceSlice wearing Alice's stylish recycled clothes.

The past sucked, so I focused on where to go next. There was no point going far since Zoroaster still had plenty more tests to run. I thought about taking the metro to my nook apartment in the Hanska Development Zone and back, but it's not like I had a lot of personal belongings to recover from a room the size of a closet.

That rental was part of dad's servitude contract – his way of making sure I always had somewhere with a bed to sleep. Not that I'd been

using it, since I'd spent most of the past year sleeping in the Luckies'
hideout in the worst part of the city.

Nah, it would make more sense to just buy some new clothes.
That would kill some time and get me moving.

I'd exhausted the amount of navigating I could do using struc-
tural landmarks, so I opened up MegaMaps in my NUI and ran
a search for clothing stores. The app automatically limited my
selection to stores in my social ranking tier, so that pretty much
meant street market stalls and recycling shops.

There were some a few blocks south of the garage, a sure sign
that Zoroaster's hideout was not in an upscale district. 'Edgerun',
it was called — a district I'd never heard of, much less ever planned
to visit.

With my epic goal set, I headed off.

Edgerun was mostly garages and tall com-crete buildings with
minimal flair – a minor industrial zone, no doubt. Zoroaster's
garage blended perfectly. On my way to the street market, I spotted
a few signs that confirmed my guess: Unicorn Brewing Co., Aero-
Dynamix, and something related to distributing Shell Shock Tacos.
All looked like small businesses trying to carve out their own little
nooks in the city. It was a shame that the best any of them could
hope for was to be absorbed by a Global Corporation.

The midday crowds were thin until I actually reached the street
market. Hundreds of colorful people packed in under shady tents
and canopies stretched from one side of the street to the other,
actively avoiding the sun. It was too early for lanterns or spotlights,
but the market still glowed with aggressive neon signs and flickering
holograms that were definitely nearing the end of their lifespans.

The marketplace smelled of fat fryers and a dozen different per-
fumes swirling together in the warm midday breeze. Walking past a

few booths and tables selling clothing, nothing caught my eye, so I continued on to the closest recycling shop.

It occupied a small storefront at the base of an apartment building, as nearly every store in the mega did unless it was part of a proper shopping center. A neon sign showing the universal symbol for a recycler, three arrows chasing each other in a circle, glowed in the window. I stepped through the open door, and the woman behind the counter greeted me with a few words and a smile.

"Only the best recycled on these shelves," she said. "Our scavers go all the way out to the red zone dump sites."

"Sounds dangerous," I said, running my hand through a rack of shirts.

"It is, but that's the only way to get high-tier recycled products. See for yourself!"

That was a subtle hint that the shop wasn't entirely above board. Corporations viewed recycling as roughly the same as eating out of the garbage, but they allowed it so that the lowest in the city could buy things they needed. A gray market industry formed around the practice, and corpos began pushing regulations through to keep it on a leash.

One of the 'rules' was that certain high-tier brands could not be scavenged and brought back into the city, while others could only be resold if their brand marks were removed – one of the main reasons many high fashion designers started printing names and labels on every inch of their products.

Naturally, the Consortium put inspectors at the dumping sites to enforce all of these rules, but they could be duped or bribed just like any corporate employ. Personal greed allowed some pretty nice stuff to make it into shops like these.

"This is a good spread," I said, feeling the woman's need for some conversation.

She smiled and nodded without taking her eyes off of me. I must have read her wrong.

Thumbing through the racks, I managed to find a gray camo-patterned hooded jacket, a pair of black leggings, and a few worthy shirts. All were in good condition and marked at prices that had to be fifty times lower than their actual value. The jacket had a big black stripe of dye painted down the sleeve – a blacked out logo, no doubt – so it was priced lower than the rest.

"Great deals," I said, plopping the armload of clothing on her counter.

Through the transparent countertop, I saw a pile of handguns and various small electronics.

"See something else you like," she asked while clerking the clothes. "You'd be surprised what people throw away. Furniture, wetgear, food…"

"Oh, not today."

I didn't want to think about the kind of food that could survive a round trip to a dump site and still be edible, but I guess some people didn't have much of a choice.

"Do you *own* a piece, dear?"

I responded with a furrowed brow.

"Hot steel. A gun, luv," the woman smiled. "You're not walking around outer districts without a gun, are you? Nice girl like you…"

The question caught me a bit off guard. When I was running jobs with the Luckies, I usually needed a gun but didn't have one. Now that I was free from them and their bond rules, the thought never hit me that I *could* have one.

"I've just…never needed one."

The woman stuffed my new clothes in a carrier bag. "All luck changes eventually. Good luck the fastest."

"That's dark, lady," I said, zipping over the payment.

She chuckled as the transaction cleared. We traded goodbyes, and I left the store with the bag in hand.

Leaving the market, I found myself thinking about what the woman said. Maybe she had a point? I'd spent a year walking around the Quarters – one of the sketchiest districts in the mega – and never had a problem. But was that because people knew I was rolling with the Luckies? Maybe there'd been an aura of protection around me that I hadn't thought about.

If so, that protection was gone, and I was just a 'nice girl' walking around alone.

The possibility drilled deeper into my brain as I covered the blocks back to Zoroaster's garage. The shadows between buildings looked a little darker than they had on my way south, as did the gazes stabbing my way from the people standing in them.

My hand kept finding its way to the hilt of the multi-knife sticking up from my belt. If one of those randos decided to come at me, would it be enough to fend them off? What if five of them decided I looked like a worthwhile target?

And what if it wasn't a rando? I wondered how many Luckies might still be alive. The kill code couldn't have flatlined *every* Lucky in the mega. If any were still alive, they might have linked me to what happened in the Quarters – which means I would be a-number-*ichi* on their most hated list.

Then I could swear I felt Monk's eyes burning a hole in the back of my head as if he himself were streaming the anxiety into my brain.

"He's dead," I whispered under my breath.

I was still grateful when Zoroaster's garage came into view. Couldn't think of a safer place than an underground shelter.

My pace quickened as I got nearer, the anxiety spurring me along. I nearly dropped my bags when a figure stirred in garage's shadow just as I was nearing the front door.

"Damn," the figure chuckled, stepping toward me. "The big man's paranoia rub off on you that fast?"

A blade of sunlight cut through the darkness he moved, revealing the shape of his grinning face like a scanner.

"Malfus," I gasped, suppressing a full-blown panic attack.

"*Mallus*," he said, still chuckling. "It means 'hammer'. Malfus is something my aunt would name a stray dog."

"Well, *hammer*. You sure are creeping around the shadows like a stray dog."

He ignored the comment and nodded toward my bags. "What'd you buy?"

"Threads. I think I might be staying here a while."

"I hope so," he said. Then he coughed and rubbed the back of his head. "You know, for your safety. I mean, I don't know much about why you're here, but *Z* doesn't arrange pickups for people unless they're in serious trouble."

I forced a smile and moved toward the door but was jolted to a stop when Mallus' hand grabbed my arm.

"Sorry..." he whispered, pulling himself closer to me. As if suddenly realizing what he'd done, he released his grip and turned both palms up. Entirely out of the shadows now, his face looked genuinely concerned.

"Look, Zoroaster also doesn't arrange pickups for people unless there's something he wants from them. I'm...not saying he's a bad guy.

But he's all about the big picture. Either you're a piece of the puzzle, or you don't exist."

"Oh, I'm a piece of the puzzle, man. That I already know. Can I go inside now?"

"Just watch your back, okay?" he said. "Not just out here. In there, too."

Stepping into the shade of the garage, I found it ironic that Mallus thought *Zoroaster* was paranoid. In a way, none of it fazed me. I'd learned to be overly cautious a long time ago. Anxiety attacks were...well, they just happened. But for the most part, I was vigilant, and that vigilance made me strong.

Reaching the red door at the back of the bay, I commed Zoroaster and asked him to let me through.

"I already got your biometrics in the system. Just use the code '7-1-7-1-9'," he said via neurocom.

I punched in the digits and leaned into the eye scanner. A second later, I was back underground, face to face with the master psycher.

Chapter Fifteen

THE NEW TEXAN

"What'd you find out?" I asked him after he waved me back into the NetOps chair.

"About the data I recovered from your brain? That's going to take me some time," he said while tapping away at a glowing slate screen. "I've been focusing on a couple of more short-term puzzles for now.

"First, figuring out more about this mysterious puck in your brain stem. And second, the events that led you here."

I narrowed my eyes at the latter.

"What about 'the events'?" I asked.

Zoroaster sat down on a rolling stool beside the NetOps chair, bringing him to my eye level.

"You told me you were handpicked by your gang leader for the handoff that brought back the Overwatch kill code."

"Yeah, I was."

"A handoff that literally anyone could have done," he said, nodding as if to agree with his own assessment. "Was there anything unusual about the way the assignment was given to you?"

"Not really," I blinked through a few memories. "I mean, it wasn't something they'd normally have me do. And Monk – the honcho – told me he'd clear my entire bond debt once it was finished."

"Really?" Zoroaster cocked his head. "I'll admit I don't know much about gang politics, but that sounds unusual. I would imagine they try to drag out those debts for as long as possible."

I nodded. "Sure. I mean, they usually wait until the bond debt is almost paid off and then, ya know, stick the poor bastard on a suicide mission. Use them as cannon fodder in some street war. Or..."

My jaw froze in the middle of my words, and the room went silent. Zoroaster let out a tiny chuckle.

"Yeah, exactly," he said. "They send them on a minor errand that they know is a setup."

"But that doesn't make sense," I said, shaking the thought from my head. "If they knew it was a setup, they wouldn't have loaded the kill code and blown their own brains out."

"Maybe," Zoroaster leaned back and rubbed his temples with latex-gloved hands. "Maybe not. It all depends on what kind of setup they thought it was. But I do have another theory. It's possible that Overwatch *wanted* you to be the courier."

"Why would they care? Anyone could have done what I did. You said it yourself."

"Jack, the agent you met. The one who gave you the kill code. Did he know anything about you?"

"Well, yeah. Associate...uhm...Goodwin. He knew a lot about me."

Zoroaster's head tilted almost imperceptibly when I said the Overwatch agent's name. Maybe I'd discovered the stoic man's 'tell'. To what end, though, I had no idea.

"But that doesn't mean anything," I added. "It's Overwatch. They check up on everybody. He probably had his buddies run my whole background while we were walking to the motel room."

Z scratched his chin, mulling over my counterargument.

"You may be right," he continued, "but it's best not to underestimate Overwatch. There are a lot of puppet masters in this world, but I dare say that none hold as many strings as they do. When the need arises, they can play those strings like an orchestra plays Mahler."

The loud metal clunk of the entry door sounded behind me, breaking Zoroaster's drifting monologue.

"That's a downright painful mixing of metaphors, big man," came a new voice from the same direction. Deep, oddly upbeat, and drowning in a drawl that belonged to lands far west of Hope Megacity. "You only do that when you're really stuck up a tree."

"Not worried, friend, just thinking," Zoroaster grinned as he rushed to meet the man with his hand outstretched.

Z's friend was was tall – still a few inches shorter than the psycher – and topped with a mane of curly blonde hair. His ready smile was every bit as scrip-bought as Zoroaster's, and he was dressed in expensive corpo-casual threads.

When he looked away from Zoroaster mid-handshake, his steely blue eyes met mine, and I sank back into my chair.

"Is that your new friend?" the man said, continuing to be too enthusiastic as he stepped in front of my chair. "Eli Wyatt McCall. Very pleased to meet you, little lady. Despite this sad, sad venue."

Zoroaster belted a laugh that I would have thought out of character for him ten minutes beforehand. He clapped Eli on the back and moved on to finishing up the introductions.

"Eli and I go back a very long time. We've remained friends through countless challenges because we share similar interests."

"Big man here calls it a 'quest for truth'," Eli interrupted. "I think of it as a 'quest for justice'."

"Revenge, he means," Zoroaster pretended to chide the man beside him. "You've no doubt noticed that Eli is what we lovingly refer to as a filthy corporate rat..."

"Hey, I dressed down for this," Eli added.

Both men laughed again before Z continued: "...but he is not a typical example of that particular rodentia."

"What?" I grimaced. "You some kind of spy?"

"Better than that," Eli smiled. "I'm a CEO. Big daddy of Western Nanofabrication ZLC, headquartered in Lonestar, New Texas."

My expression made it clear that I'd never heard of the company.

"Eli's company manufactures parts," said Zoroaster. "Processors, interlinks, servos, neural net fibers...pretty much anything you can imagine. And they provide those parts to every Global Corporation that operates factories in Hope or Lonestar."

"That makes me the leading expert on figuring out unexplained corpo tech," added Eli as he tucked a few locks of golden hair behind an ear. "At least, the leading expert that this bastard is going to get to cooperate with him."

"You want to look at my puck, then?" I asked. "You're not cutting it out of my head, you know."

"No, no, sweetheart! No way," Eli held up both hands. "Transdermal imaging. I just need to see shapes, outlines, pathways. Etchings or stampings, if there are any. That sort of thing."

"We're hoping Eli will see enough rare or unusual components that he can add some pieces to the puzzle. Maybe which lab assembled the unit, or even figure out how to access old design schematics."

I aimed a concerned stare at Zoroaster for a good minute before I locked eyes with Eli.

"Why should I trust you? I get that you're friends with Z, but you're still a corpo. Why wouldn't you just turn me over to Tao-Com or Overwatch? I'm sure that would earn you a new car or move you up a floor on whatever Skypillar you live in."

"Young lady," Eli grinned. "I don't want to live in a Skypillar any more than those dandies want me living in one. That is a club where I am *not* welcome, and I'm glad for it."

"Eli has a tenuous relationship with the Global Corporations," Zoroaster added. "Besides bringing a lot of unwelcome New Texas swagger into the boardroom, he's deceptively cunning with his business deals. They can't figure him out, but they can't run their factories without his products."

"And many have tried to buy me out. Someone, probably High-Castle, even tried to have me killed once. Once *that I know of.* And the more I carry on in this city, the more I hate everything about the way they run it."

"Can't you just go back to New Texas? What's wrong with the mega there?"

"Lonestar is a jewel in the desert, I'll give you that. But Hope is like the corpo proving ground for testing new and better ways to screw over the average citizen. When something works here, it don't take long for it to spread to the other cities. As far as I'm concerned, this place is 'patient zero' of the corpo-rat plague, right Doc?"

Eli nudged Zoroaster in the elbow.

"Right. A diseased society, diseased class system, diseased minds...whatever maladies originate here affect the rest of the world when left unchecked."

"Lonestar is just Hope 2.0, then?" I asked.

"It's well on its way," Eli said, no longer smiling. "And I aim to stop that. With the big man's help, of course. And yours, Jack."

I devoted another moment to weighing my options before finally nodding my approval. We were all equally clueless about the puck, the BeanStalk, the Overwatch kill code, and where I fit into any of it. Might as well work together for some answers.

Zoroaster got to setting up his imaging device while I wondered about my end game. Maybe the reason I didn't feel like I had choices was because I wasn't sure what my next steps should be – much less my final destination.

You can't pick between turning left or turning right if you don't know where you're going.

I came to Zoroaster for help, but the more I thought about it, the more it felt like I was being drawn into his game rather than being given a solution to my problems. Sure enough, I had a place to hide, but I couldn't imagine a long-term outcome that worked in my favor.

Those thoughts kept me busy while the psycher and the CEO worked, running imaging scans on the back of my head and whispering back and forth over the results. It seemed like hours had passed when they finally brought me back into the conversation.

"Well, Jack, Eli thinks he has enough clues to work from," Zoroaster said, waving me out of the NetOps chair and pointing to a screen on the far wall. "Take a look."

The monitor showed a handful of scan results, each looking like technical schematics surrounded by the shadows of my neck and skull.

The transdermal imager had rendered perfect cross-sections of the puck implant from at least six different angles.

"Most of the components are off-the-shelf," Eli waved toward the images. "The casing, bioneural interfaces, insulation, cooling system – pretty much all stock parts we ship by the thousands for assembling neurocom devices. Or at least we did twenty years ago…some of these exact parts are obsolete now."

He poked his finger at a rendering of the puck that clearly showed its location in my spinal cord.

"There's two interesting things about this implant. The first is the most obvious: the placement. Right into the spinal column. Very strange for tech that was around when you were born."

"And what's the other thing?" I asked.

"The quantity of bio-neural interfaces and how they're connected. I see at least ten times the number of interfaces that would be usable by a bit of wetgear from that generation. One that size, anyway. And your cybernetics aren't connected directly to your neurocom mesh like a typical install. They run through the puck. Never seen anything like it."

Zoroaster stepped up the monitor and gestured toward a different image. This rendering showed a large white hexagon in the center of one of the cross-sections.

"Which leads us to the mystery within the mystery," Zoroaster said. "This chip. Pretty obvious that it's the processor, but it's the one component that Eli can't even make a guess on."

Eli nodded and folded his arms. "You said this puck was installed by TaoCom, so I'd bet my fattest Holstein that the core is one-hundred-dred-percent hush-hush Chinatech."

"That's great, guys," I said. "But – no offense – you haven't learned anything I didn't already know. Or at least kind of assumed."

Zoroaster grinned and clapped a hand on my shoulder.

"Not every expedition leads to Solomon's city," he said. "Sometimes you just find another patch of jungle."

With that, he began switching off monitors and packing away his imaging hardware.

"That's enough exploring for today, Jack," he said, looking up from his tools. "You can head back out or get some more rest. Don't forget your bags here. Maybe you should try on your new clothes."

I smiled at the two men, snatching my bags from the floor before heading into the bunker's sleeping area. The door clanked shut behind me before I remembered it could only be opened from the outside.

Setting my bags down on my cot, I glanced over to the intercom panel near the door. Like tumblers falling into place in an old mechanical lock, my apprehensions kicked over into a realization.

What Mallus had said outside – that Zoroaster was probably in this for his own good – hadn't left my thoughts. And I still wasn't sure how anyone could trust Eli if he was in bed with all the major corps. The anxious energy shot through me like a switch had been tripped, and my arms and legs were moving in an instant.

Pocket interfacer in hand, I quietly pulled open the panel of the intercom and touched leads to wires on a multicolored pigtail. The intercom was old-school analog tech, but using my 'facer as a multimeter, I figured out the purpose of each wire based on resistance and amperage.

I would need to patch a few of the wires together. The synthetic fingernails on my wetgear arm made for good wire strippers, so scraping insulation was easy. Then a few twists of copper brought the correct wires together.

My 'facer was already synced to my NUI, so I just had to touch the leads to the right bare wires...

...and boom. I was using the intercom system as an audio pick-up and streaming it right into my brain. Eli and Zoroaster were still talking in the main room.

"...not sure. If the device controls her limbic system *and* is isolated from her neurocom, it could have kept her alive."

That was Eli. Then Zoroaster chimed in:

"Well, based on her medical history, I'd imagine the entire purpose of the puck was, for lack of a better term, integrated life support. Some augmentation to her nervous system to correct a number of birth defects."

"Look, Doc. I know these corpos better than anyone, and that doesn't track. People like you and me might not think this way, but I don't see how there's enough profit in saving...what? Damaged newborns? TaoCom wouldn't spend a dime on that kind of research. Especially at this level."

"Sounds like you do think that way," Zoroaster said flatly.

"Come on. You know what I mean. Advanced tech. *Secret* tech. They'd be putting it in...I dunno. Satellites or mech infantry suits. Not some newborn girl from street level. Even for testing, that doesn't fit."

The room fell silent long enough that I glanced at my 'facer to make sure I was still connected. Then Zoroaster's voice continued:

"There's something else. Right before you came in. She told me the name of the Overwatch agent that gave her the kill code – the cyber-somatic hack that wiped out her gang. It was Goodwin."

"No shit," Eli said, the accompanying chuckle more apprehensive than jovial this time. "One of yours, wasn't he? I'm guessing you didn't expect him to be running around melting neurocoms."

"No. Which means he isn't playing by the rules. Especially since I'm fairly certain it was *my* kill code he used."

I dropped the leads and stood frozen by the doorway. The only sound now was the insanely fast beating in my chest.

I downed a cold drink from the vending machine and waited for myself to chill out. I was smart enough to know that I had one advantage in this game, and I was going to play it.

For one reason or another, Zoroaster needed me. For now, that meant a little safety was guaranteed – which was more than I would have on the street.

Holding that small comfort in the front of my mind, I climbed into my cot for another long sleep. It didn't come easy, even with my neurocom's Bedtime Mode tweaking my adenosine, melatonin, and serotonin levels.

But eventually, the warm rising waters of sleep managed to drown my anxious thoughts.

The *LucidSleep* logo in the center of my vision told me I'd finally drifted off. The lack of any real feeling in my body confirmed it – as did my surroundings.

Again, I was in my childhood apartment. There was the crutch, the couch, and the terminal with my schoolwork on it. A rerun?

I considered changing the dreamscape into something more interesting. Maybe a relaxing setting, like a forest or a beach. Then the door chime sounded, and I knew Allie was probably about to walk in.

"Front door, open," I said, mainly out of habit.

The door slid into the wall, but it wasn't Allie standing on the other side. The hallway lights flickered across blue hair and too-perfect synthskin.

"Gina?" I said, jumping to my feet.

The girl's slender legs cut a path toward me. Blue lips and trendy hair left the shadows of the doorway behind as she approached.

It was every bit Gina, or my best memory of her, and I got a little excited thinking it might turn into one of *those* dreams. Her intense gray eyes measured me with every step she took, and the fire in them made me think – or maybe hope – that she approved.

But the closer she got, the more I noticed the look of concern that didn't match what I'd seen on the street outside Cloud Seven.

"Jack," she said just as she stopped an arm's length away. "You're not safe."

"Hm. I'm guessing you're my subconscious in this one? Or my anxieties? Either way, I already know I'm not safe."

"He's not dead," Gina continued. "And he's looking for you."

"What? Who?"

She slowly raised her arm and pointed behind me.

"Him."

I turned around, and my heart nearly stopped when my eyes landed on a tall, muscled man covered in tattoos. I jumped back, crashing into Gina, and stared wide-eyed at the sentient slab of meat.

His face was limp and lifeless, like it melted in the sun, and his eyes were white like a dead man's. He stood over me, frozen, but his inked chest swelled and released with each of his slow breaths.

Monk. It was him, apparently ravaged by the kill code but not dead. And those cadaverous white eyes couldn't hide how much anger was behind them.

He didn't move. I blinked and leaned forward, looking into his destroyed face. Monk's mouth didn't so much as twitch, but I heard his voice in my head. Just words, hateful words, floating into my mind:

Liar. Traitor. Murderer. Corpo rat...

I shuddered when Gina's hand touched my shoulder from behind. "He's looking for you," she whispered, and I jolted from my sleep.

Chapter Sixteen

TRUST

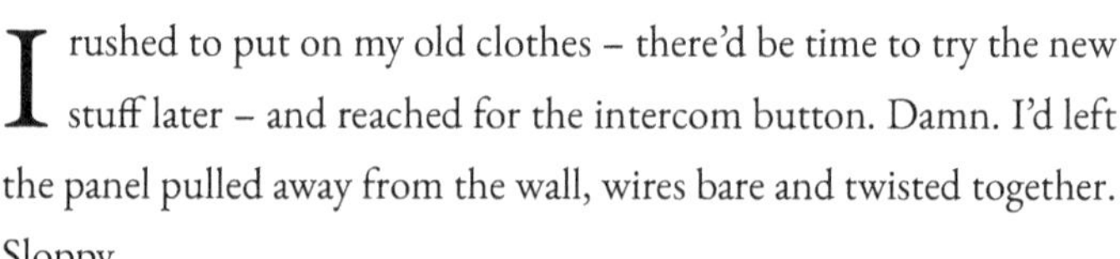

I rushed to put on my old clothes – there'd be time to try the new stuff later – and reached for the intercom button. Damn. I'd left the panel pulled away from the wall, wires bare and twisted together. Sloppy.

I shoved the whole mess back into place and pressed the call button. Nothing. And again. No reply.

"Skitz," I hissed.

"Zoroaster!" I yelled, turning to the new plan of banging my carbon fiber fist against the door until someone answered.

A few seconds later, the door popped open, and Mallus leaned in with a curious look on his face.

"Geez, you okay?" he asked. "You know there's an intercom, right?"

"I broke it," I said, pushing my way past him. "Where's Z? I think someone sent me a...secret message. While I was sleeping."

Mallus gave the busted intercom panel a quizzical look, then followed me into the main room. "Shouldn't be possible, Jack. Z's neurocom cracks make you a ghost on the network."

"Then he didn't do 'em right," I said.

Mallus chuckled. "Don't let him hear you say that," he added. "Look, maybe someone with skills got through. Who do you think sent the message? Another psycher like Z?"

"No. Just some girl I met once."

Mallus shrugged. "I've had dreams about girls I've 'met once', and they sure as hell weren't secret messages."

I shot him a disapproving look. He was shaping up to be one of those people who didn't take anything seriously. I didn't like those people.

"Dude, what did you do to this thing?" Mallus called out from the bunkroom corridor after turning his attention back to the intercom panel.

The question made me think of what I had done...and more specifically, what I'd heard.

"Mallus, can I trust Z? Like *really* trust him?"

"As long you don't forget what I said before," he replied. "Why?"

"Don't screw with me. I can't shake the feeling that all this is too convenient. And that I'm being used somehow."

"You know how street kids get so used to things being bad they can't understand why anything would be good?" Mallus asked. "That's you right now."

"So I'm just 'a naive street kid', then?"

Mallus finished messing with the intercom panel and closed it back up. He keyed the button and spoke into it. "That's not what I meant," his voice echoed through the speakers in the NetOps room.

I rolled my eyes.

"You think I'm from some exec family?" he continued, the frustration on his face turning to something more grim. "My mom worked at a stall selling refurb appliances. And my dad...well. If he wasn't blacked out in some bar, he would hack the pay terminals on vending machines."

"But now?" I asked.

"They both died years ago. From the contaminated water in Golden Gate back when that all went down."

"I'm sorry."

He looked away, closed his eyes for a long few seconds. "The point I was getting at is that I know where you're at right now. Not knowing how to trust anybody. Figuring everything good is just there to get your hopes up before something else goes to skitz."

I nodded. Maybe he could take *some* things seriously. He certainly nailed my current mind state. A moment passed before we both realized we were just staring blankly at each other, then Mallus coughed and shook his head.

"I *do* trust Z," he said. "But it took time for me to get there. What I can tell you is that I know you're safe here. And if that changes, I'll be the first to tell you."

"Thanks, Mallus."

The sound of an opening hatch punctuated my gratitude. Z stepped in through the sally port, sealing the hatch behind him.

"Oh no," he grinned. "What has this guy been saying about me?"

I looked at Mallus, then back to the smiling psycher in his long duster. "Good things," I said. "But listen, I think I have a problem. I think I got a warning message in my dream last night."

Z looked thoughtful for a moment, then walked toward the NetOps chair.

"Unlikely, but not impossible," he said. "Someone with the right skills could still locate your neurocom on the MiFi network. Are you sure it was a message?"

"Pretty damn sure," I sidestepped the NetOps chair and sat on the stool that Zoroaster usually used. "It was someone I met recently. Someone that worked for the Luckies. She told me that Monk isn't dead and that he's looking for me."

I glanced back at Mallus, but he was elbow-deep in a stack of network hardware, intent on finishing whatever he was doing before I pulled him away.

"And Monk was the man who actually slotted the isostick with the kill code. Is that right?" Z asked.

"Yeah, he did it right in front of me. Then I pretty much watched him fall to the ground with blood coming out of his ears."

"Then he's dead."

"How do you know?" I asked, realizing I had an opening for the perfect probe. "It's not like you wrote the kill code. You don't know how it works."

I stole a glance at Mallus. He'd stopped working again and was looking at me from the corner of his eye.

Z stopped pacing, and sat beside me in the NetOps chair.

"I know enough from seeing the residual code in your scans. He couldn't have survived. The kill code sends repeating false signals into the brain through every active bio-neural channel. It kicks off a stress cascade in the tissues leading to severe damage. Seizure, stroke, aneurysm. With enough active channels, it would make your brain hemorrhage right out of your nose."

"What if there aren't any bio-neural channels at all?" I asked. "Monk was a total organic. He didn't have any wetgear."

"Oh," Zoroaster mulled that over for a second. "Well, he had a neurocom. He couldn't have loaded the stick without it. That alone should be enough active channels to get the desired effect."

"Should be?"

"It's like you said." Zoroaster grinned. "It's not like I wrote it."

My eyes narrowed at that, and I could tell Z noticed. Was this guy playing mental chess with me or something? An annoying thought considering Mallus had just done a hell of a job convincing me not to worry about it.

"You're safe down here, regardless," Z continued. "Why don't you go take a shower and change into clean clothes. I've got some data to run through with you, and then we can talk about options."

"Options?" I asked.

"It can wait. Just go shower. And eat if you haven't already."

Not the worst suggestion, so I went along with it. After saying 'bye' to Mallus, I returned to the bunk area of the fallout shelter and closed the hatch behind me.

I washed up in the bunkroom shower, thoroughly enjoying it after days of accumulating grime. After drying off with a towel from the nearby supply, I changed into my new clothes: black leggings, a burnt orange shirt long enough to work as a dress, and the gray camo hooded jacket. I buckled the belt with my sheathed MMK over the top, and pulled on my trusty surplus ankle boots.

When I came back into the main room, Mallus was gone, and Z was back to his usual pacing with the long neural interface cable tethering his head to the NetOps chair. The man was definitely not afraid of hard work and long hours.

"Look, Zoroaster. Monk dreams aside, I can't stay down here forever. I can't go back to the ganger scene, and I'm not safe around corpos. I need to know what's next."

Z smiled and waved me over to the desk terminal. I joined him.

"That's what I wanted to talk about. We're fast approaching a crossroads where you need to make a choice. Once we've learned what we can about the BeanStalk, I can get you out of Hope Megacity.

"The safest plan would be to exfiltrate you to Cascadia Megacity on the west coast. New identity, new start."

I wasn't ready to leave Hope. I shook my head. "What else you got?"

"You also need to know that a security bulletin went out this morning from TaoCom," he continued. "It identifies you by name in connection with an attempted breach of an extremely secure asset."

"Skitz."

"Don't worry, it changes nothing for right now. It just means you're going to have a hard time assimilating back into the population if you decide to stay."

"Meaning?"

"Meaning if you don't exfiltrate, you're going to be living underground for the rest of your life in Hope." He gestured absently above his head. "Not literally. But you..."

"Yeah," I cut him off. "I get it. So I'll be OTG forever."

"At least for the foreseeable future. Corporations have long reaches and longer memories. But don't worry...I'm a bit of an expert off-grid living. And you won't have to be alone."

"I hope that doesn't mean living down here in the cot next to yours," I said.

Zoroaster laughed.

"I don't live down here. You've just got me working a lot. I have a pretty nice apartment, off the books, naturally. We'll get you one, too. If you still choose to stay."

I leaned back in the chair and stared at a wall of blinking lights for a long minute.

"Running doesn't seem right. My gut is telling me to stay."

Zoroaster clapped his hands together and flashed his perfect corpo teeth. I knew when he did that, I'd just done or said whatever he was hoping for. It made me think about that old scientist who trained dogs with a bell...

"Okay, Jack. This means a change in curriculum. You're not just my guinea pig now; you're a part of the team – and we need to get you equipped for survival as a shadow citizen."

"I was your guinea pig?" I asked through a glare tinted with second thoughts.

"Just a joke," he smiled. "But listen, I'm still digging into this security alert. I'd like to find out where TaoCom got their intel, in case there are any leaks we need to know about. Have you told anyone outside of this room about what you're seeing? Or about contacting me?"

Should I lie about Allie? He'll probably think I'm a smoothbrain for spilling my secrets to a Global Corporation employ.

No, I shouldn't hide it. Better to come clean.

"Before we met...before I even knew about you, I told someone that I was seeing...the green thing. Her name's Alice. She's actually the one who said I should try to find you because you might know something about it."

Zoroaster narrowed his eyes. "Told you to find *me*? How did she even know about me?"

"Another security bulletin that mentioned you. Just by your hacker name. It didn't seem like they knew anything about you..."

"They? As in...a corporation? Does this friend *work* for a corporation?"

"TaoCom employ, yeah. She's a researcher. Level four, I think she said."

Zoroaster resumed pacing from wall to wall, stopping every few steps to rub the back of his head or temples in alternating fashion. He seemed to dip in and out of awareness, probably splitting his brain power between the conversation and whatever he was doing on the DarkNet.

"More coincidences or blind luck?" he muttered to himself.

"I...don't know how Allie would be anything more than a coincidence."

Zoroaster turned on his heels and looked square into my eyes.

"Look at the chain of events. The gang chooses *you* to send to Overwatch and grab the kill code. You somehow survive the kill code, and the aftermath leads you to BeanStalk. BeanStalk leads you to your friend – a TaoCom employ. She tells you to find me, a threat they're clearly looking for."

"You think I set you up?" I growled.

"No, no. Not at all. I think this all seems a little too orchestrated, but not by your hand. I need to check in on your friend. What's her full name?"

"What do you mean, 'check up'? You're not going to black bag her, interrogate her...none of that?"

"Of course not. I just need to look at her data. Her recent coms."

"Promise? Like a serious promise?"

"Yes," Zoroaster said, putting out his hand to shake. "Only data mining. No black bags or interrogations."

No options. As usual.

"Alice Krieger," I said. "And I'm holding you to what you said, Z."

We shook hands. He nodded.

After a minute, I added: "To recap, I had nothing to do with setting any of this up. I hope talking to Allie didn't make things worse."

"I take a lot of precautions for a reason, Jack. Even if that was a setup to lead TaoCom to me, it didn't work. I had decoys. Multiple vans going to different parts of the city, and all of them with eyes open for surveillance. I even had a few false pickups and exchanges with dupes."

"Dupes...of me?"

"Yes. Phantom work." Zoroaster grinned. "After Mallus dropped you here, he drove Tandy to the other side of town, and dropped her at a metro station right in front of an HMPD camera. By the time she got out of the van, she had already cloned your neurocom ID and 3D-printed a Jack mask to spoof the facial recognition software.

"That happened two more times with different dupes. As far as the watchers are concerned, you ended up in three different places by the end of the day."

"Hell of an operation," I said.

"Make no mistake, we're not mercs, and we're not gangers," the psycher crossed his arms. "We're not operating on Overwatch level, but we've got resources. If we didn't, keeping you here in the mega wouldn't even be an option."

Where were Z's resources coming from, considering the only people with resources to spare were corpos? For that matter, how big of a crew was he running? I thought Zoroaster had a few kids driving vans and running on rooftops, but it was starting to sound like he was fielding a shadow army.

"I can tell by that look, you have many questions," Zoroaster proffered. "And since you're staying with us, you'll get answers."

His eyes flashed as he zipped an address into my NUI. A bar about fifteen blocks away.

"I want you to meet some of the others in this crew," he added. "Learn about what we do, and start making friends with the people who are going to have your back from now on. I've got someone coming to drive you over there.

"When you get back, I'll update you on what I've been able to dig out of the data you brought me."

"Anything good?" I asked.

"Just pieces that need assemblage," he said, pointing to the cable running from the side of his head. "You should head topside. Your ride will be here shortly."

Chapter Seventeen

THE STREET KIDS

I could feel Z's eyes on me all the way to the exit hatch. After climbing the stairs and popping out of the red door, I was met by Mallus and a somewhat-familiar girl about my age. She wore a pink and teal bodcon dress over a layer of fine white fishnet covering her from neck to feet. Trendy compared to Mallus, who looked like he still hadn't changed out his black and gray casuals – perfect for a morning jog in Castle Park or a busy day of covert ops.

"Jack," Mallus called out. "We're your wheels. You remember Tandy? She was in the back of the van..."

"Snatch and grab," I said through a fleeting grin. "And I hear you wore my face for a little while."

Tandy smirked. She wasn't even slightly intimidating without the hood and half-mask. Pale, freckled skin and puffy cheeks gave her a child-like look. It was marred by an angular scar running from her forehead to her right cheek – most likely the install marks of an ocular implant. Her pink hair was cut too short to cover it.

"I've worn worse," she said. "At least you're cute. It's when I have to look like a fifty-year-old chung with a beard that it starts to get weird."

"Alright," Mallus cut in. "Let's get rollin'. A few more waiting for us at the spot."

Mallus thumbed toward an Edison sedan visible through the open garage door. The candy paint job reflected the sun like a flawless mirror, changing color from black to purple as we got closer. Mallus' eyes flashed blue and all four doors slid onto the roof, revealing a white synth leather interior.

"Traded in the van?" I asked.

Mallus climbed in the driver's seat, and Tandy pointed me toward the passenger door. She climbed into the back.

The upholstery responded as soon I dropped into the ride, adjusting gel bladders to perfectly conform the seat to my body.

"Don't get used to it," Mallus said, starting the engine. "We don't hold on to cars for very long."

"Yup, everything gets traced eventually," Tandy added, sinking deep into the back seat. "This will probably be in the junkpile in a couple of weeks after we glaze it into little bitty pieces."

Glaze. Usually that meant using corpo-grade garnet lasers manufactured in orbit. If they really had one, it could probably slice the whole car into pocket-sized chunks in about ten seconds. Just another one of Z's 'resources' that seemed too good to be true.

"Sucks," Mallus muttered, running his hand over the center touch console before punching the throttle. "Some rides you just don't want to part with, feel me?"

I couldn't blame him. The Edison rode like it was on rails. I doubt the ARVs flying over our heads could even run that smooth. The car also had serious hardware under the hood – Mallus made no effort to hide its performance. He was all throttle, and the car accelerated so quickly that the whole drive felt like a single pass down a drag strip, even when he was forced to stop for traffic lights and crosswalks full of pedestrians.

Checking the clock on my NUI, I saw the entire trip took a total of nine minutes. Not bad for crossing a district at midday. Mallus whipped the sedan into a parking garage, and the three of us piled out.

"Here we go," he said, yanking a few devices from his pockets.

He tossed a palm-sized flat disc under the car, then hid another device inside the rear wheel well. He slapped the last object onto the registration tag on the back of the car, and the blocky ID scanner code changed into a new configuration of little black squares.

"That's a rolling tag spoofer. Then there's the immobilizer, and, uh...the tracking jammer," Mallus said, pointing first at the wheel well, then under the car.

"Do we need all of it all the time? Prolly not," he shrugged. "But ya know. Pays to be...on guard."

Tandy laughed. "He never did this much to protect a van," she said, slapping me on the arm. "C'mon, Mal, you know you're in love."

Mallus glanced at me, then back at the Edison, his face going pink as it twitched.

"Hey," he scowled back at Tandy. "Don't knock a man for appreciating a tight ride."

The implication made me skip a step, and I could tell Mallus regretted saying it as soon as the words came out. His eyes snapped open so wide they looked like they might fall out of his skull, then he turned another shade of pink and froze.

Tandy's chuckles turned into a roaring laugh that nearly dropped her to the floor of the parking garage. She tried to pile on another cutting remark, but couldn't catch her breath to do it.

Our wheelman composed himself, took a breath, and shot me an apologetic look. "Sorry. That's...you know what I meant."

"We all did, you chungus!" Tandy was still laughing it up. "C'mon, let's get there already."

She slapped us both on the back as she slipped between, legging it for the lift down to street level. Mallus and I followed.

Street level was buzzing. Two tricked cars were parked on the sidewalk nearby, each competing to drown out the other's music. Peeps danced and threw back cans and bottles all around the noise.

Two muscled-out and geared-up bros traded punches to the face in the street near it all. One had a pair of chrome arms that flashed in the light whenever he swung. The other guy's arms were synthskin, but a large patch of the fleshy covering had been ripped away from his shoulder, exposing the wetgear workings.

"Kinda hot, right? Give it a minute," Tandy said, grabbing my shoulder. "The guns'll come out. I'll bet that guy is uber pissed his fancy gear got scuffed."

I heard Mallus scraping his feet on the sidewalk behind us, seemingly uninterested.

"Let's move before this goes syndrome," he said after a minute, pointing a sneaky gesture into the alley behind us.

Tandy stepped to it and pulled me along by the shoulder.

"Pfft. I'm so used to phantom duty that I forget you nuds have to *try* to go unseen," Tandy said, letting go of me and returning to her usual giddy stride.

"Yeah, you're a real ghost, Tan," Mallus quipped, making a point of looking her outfit up and down.

"I blend, bud," she smirked back, then twirled. "Hiding in plain sight, see?"

"At least Jack has a little style," she winked back at me. "Don't be like mister monochrome here. He thinks 'black ops' is a dress code."

For the first time in a while, I laughed. How long had it been? Days? Not since I saw Allie, at least. And those laughs weren't great because I was half-drowning in fear at the time. Now I wasn't drowning. I felt oddly safe.

But I jumped when three gunshots echoed down the alley from where we came. Then quite a few more.

"Told ya," Tandy said. "Aaaaand here we are."

She stopped at an unmarked service entrance, her eyes flashing green for an instant, then she pushed the door open wide.

"After you, lovelies!"

I followed Mallus into a dim hallway. Looking back at Tandy, she was still leaning out of the doorway, trying to catch a glimpse at the gunfight – transfixed, and biting her bottom lip.

"Uhm, Tandy?" I said, slowing my walk. "You coming?"

"Not yet..." she said without moving. "Grrr...alright. I can't see anything from here anyway. Boo."

She shut the door, sealing out the light. The hallway turned from dim to black. My NUI adjusted my visual gamma accordingly, but it made little difference, and I slammed my carbon fiber knee into something jutting from the wall.

The upshot of my old, crappy wetgear was that the pain receptors were pretty worn out. The organic knee would have hurt a hell of a lot more.

"Come on, ya goon," Tandy laughed, then forged ahead to make sure I didn't trip and kill myself.

Chapter Eighteen

THE LOWLIFE

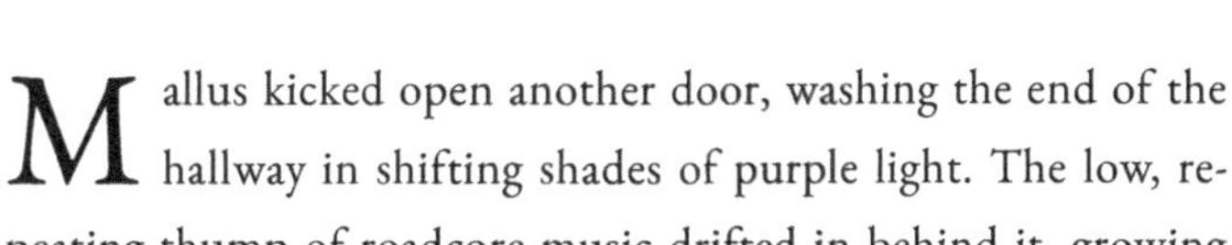

Mallus kicked open another door, washing the end of the hallway in shifting shades of purple light. The low, repeating thump of roadcore music drifted in behind it, growing into an obnoxious drum-heavy blitz as we all stepped into a definite dive bar.

"*Brainhammer*," Mallus shouted to me over the music. "Good song."

I replied with a very unconvincing half nod, then scoped out the venue. The purple lights thoroughly painted the room's interior, just large enough for half a dozen pub tables and a two-meter bar at the far wall. Monitors behind the bar played ads for various liquors while actual bottles of the stuff lined the shelves around them.

A lone bartender leaned against the wall under a neon sign spelling out "LOWLIFE BAR AND VEND" in a flowing script. She was clearly bored with the handful of patrons scattered around nursing their drinks.

"Kinda dead," Mallus added, still shouting over the music.

"Can't imagine why," I replied, knowing there was no way he could hear me.

Tandy took the lead and navigated us through the pub tables to a side doorway. The sign above it showed restrooms to the left and vending to the right. We went right.

That took us through an even smaller room full of vending machines advertising everything from NuBurritos and Chug Cola to cybernetic accessories and entertainment isosticks. Sticks were available with games and vids – natch there were hardcore XXX versions of both on offer.

Through the vending area, another door. Tandy held it open, but Mallus pinged my neurocom with a call before I could step through.

"Don't mention Zoroaster or anything you've been working on with him," his voice sounded in my head when I accepted the com. "And don't be too nervous. These guys are on our side."

"Roger," I thought back before closing the com.

Mallus nodded, then ushered me through the door into a large stockroom with more square footage than the bar at the end of the hall. Metal shelves loaded with boxes and bottles lined the walls, but the minimal light made it hard to see details.

A single shaft of light from a ventilation duct in the ceiling cut through the darkness enough for me to see that the center of the room was cleared out to make room for a couch, a small table, and a random mix of bar stools and metal chairs.

There was no thumping music now, only the silence of three strangers staring at me from their seats.

Tandy shut the door and announced: "I bring you...the new blood!"

The strangers didn't so much as twitch. I was frozen, unsure of what to say next.

"This is Jack," Mallus chimed in, urging me further into the room by poking me in the back.

I committed and moved toward the strangers, a fist-sized lump growing in my throat.

They said nothing while I tried to size them up through the mottled rays of overhead light. To my left sat a blonde woman in a charcoal GreySec uniform, minus the helmet. Her bullet-stopper vest was undone, allowing her to lounge far enough back into the couch that most of her face was cloaked in shadows.

A chair on my right was occupied by a slim man in a fashionable purple and white suit – not so much corpo style as something a big-scrip showoff might wear to a club.

The most notable of the trio was straight ahead of me, dead large and completely in silhouette. Even sitting in a chair, I imagined they had to be the tallest person in the mega. Definitely the bulkiest. I might as well have been looking at an inkblot of a ten-ton truck.

"'Sup?" I asked, wondering which would engage me first.

"Alright," the suited man said, rising to his feet to bow his head.

His voice was thick with a Briton's accent, and he was just a bit too lanky, a bit too tall, and his eyes bulged just a bit too much.

"Pleasure, Jack. Blokes call me 'Pilky'."

He then raised an open palm to the shadowy truck-person to his right.

"This 'ere is Vikk. Man of very few words but many talents."

Just then, Tandy strode past me and sat on the arm of the giant's chair. The contrast in their sizes made him look all that more inhuman.

"Vikk is a full-spec golem," she chirped before leaning in to kiss him on the cheek. "But he's all heart."

"No matter that he no longer *has* a heart," Pilky added with a chuckle and a deferring hand gesture.

Vikk's head turned slightly toward the Brit before emitting a digitized-sounding grunt.

"Only takin' the piss, mate," Pilky said, grinning.

Outside of elite corpo military groups, Golems were as rare as blue unicorns. Almost complete cybernetic retrofits. Some of them were little more than a human brain in a high-powered wetgear body. It explained how he could be so monstrously large.

I nodded in acknowledgment and forced out a smile, but I still couldn't tell if the big silhouetted 'bloke' was even looking at me.

"And I'm Katarina Guterres," the woman to my left cut in. "We've met."

She leaned forward, her GreySec gear shifting as she rested her elbows on her knees. Her face fully in the light, I could remember her sharp features from somewhere.

"Still have that Sevenex MMK on your belt," she grinned, nodding at my knife.

The Promenade! She was the cop that questioned me right next to the BeanStalk before I knew it was the BeanStalk.

"Uh, hello again," I patted the knife on my belt. "Yeah, still got it."

"Good," Katarina said, "because I brought you a gift."

She reached down to a black duffel next to her leg, pulled out a foot-long ruggedized case, and set it on the table between us.

"Sit down, open it up," she added, waving me toward an empty chair.

I sat, but not without noticing that Mallus was nowhere to be seen. He must have slipped out behind me during the introductions.

Leaning forward in my chair, I slid the drab green polymer case close and ran my fingers over the engraved metal placard on the lid:

SevenArms Research, GC

Distributed by SevenArms Hope Megacity, ZLC

Manufactured in Oceania, Protecting Your World

No way...

I popped the compression latch on the lid and opened the case.

"MMK cartridges," I smiled. "Holy skitz."

"They're easy enough for a GreySec patrol captain to requisition," Katarina said, sinking back into the couch. "I figured you'd have a hard time getting these."

Neurotoxin cartridge, shock cartridge, plasma blade cartridge with emitter rail...and a few that I didn't even know by the labels. I'd have to look these over later. I secured the poly container's lid and set the treasure on my lap.

"Yeah, try impossible. Thanks, really."

"Likely you'll need 'em," Pilky said, lowering himself gracefully back into his chair before crossing his legs.

"For starters," a deep, digitized voice rasped from the shadows ahead. Vikk, finally speaking up. Few words, as advertised.

Katarina nodded her agreement. "Our mutual friend sent us some specs on your hardware, and we're supposed to take you...shopping."

"Ohhhh, shopping trip," Tandy said from the arm of Vikk's chair. "I knew I tagged along for a reason!"

"Kitted out is more like it," added Pilky, turning to grin at Tandy. "Cyberware, firearms, body armor. Sorry, luv. Only the essentials."

"Black market shopping trip! Even better," Tandy giggled.

I tilted my head. "Why do I need any of that?"

I wanted to mention that I was probably spending the foreseeable future locked up in Z's bomb shelter, but then I remembered Mallus' warning about keeping his name out of it.

"Two things," Katarina replied. "First, you're helping out our friend with his research, but our organization is always short-handed, so you're going to have to earn your keep sooner or later; second, you've got useful skills."

Katarina took a long drink from a bottle of Samwise Beer. "This isn't about putting you to work for the sake of it. We can really use what you've got. I don't want you to think of this like corpo servitude or some lowlife ganger bond – we're a team."

"There are benefits, mind," Pilky said. "You'll see."

"And benefits have to be earned, Jack," Katarina continued. "Ten years at my corpo job have made me a good judge of character, and I've got a positive feeling about you. But I also need to see you step up, prove yourself as an operator."

"Operator, huh?" I asked.

"Part of our little...society in the shadows. Think of it this way. Over five hundred years ago, the waters just off the coast were teeming with pirates. You know the stories. Thieves, murderers, every nasty type you can think of.

But they were also sailors and military men tired of the status quo. They had stories, lives, families. In time, those pirates controlled the seas around the New World, and you know how they got to that point?"

"Not really," I answered.

"By being professionals. By rising above goonery and uniting for something bigger than the next haul of coins or bottle of rum. The most powerful pirates didn't just run a ship; they commanded *fleets* of ships. And these pirate societies were more fair and democratic than most nations would be for hundreds of years after those men died."

"So being a good operator..." I said slowly, "...is about being professional. Being part of the bigger society."

Katarina nodded. "I grew up as a street kid. I know what it's like believing that you only have two choices for rising above mediocrity:

serve a corporation or join a gang. We're the third choice. The best choice."

"Somewhere in the middle, huh?" I grinned.

"In a way," Pilky laughed.

Then Tandy jumped down from the arm of the chair and bounced over to me.

"History. Fun. Okay, you chungs, Jack's on board – I can tell. Let's get to the good part!" She put her hand on my shoulder, "You with me, girl?"

I looked to Katarina, Pilky, and Vikk for a clue to the right answer. They were silent and unreadable.

"Ready if you are," I shrugged.

All three of my new buddies rose out of their seats at the same time. Katarina snapped her body armor closed and tightened a few straps around her waist. Pilky brushed the wrinkles out of his pants and picked an invisible something from his sleeve before flicking it away.

Then Vikk stood with a mechanical whir, his head nearly touching the ceiling.

"Ready," he said in his monotone, digitized voice.

Chapter Nineteen

THE RDZ

Luckily for Vikk, the storeroom had a large roll-up door on the far wall. Actually, I don't think it was luck. It's probably why they used the storeroom as a hangout in the first place.

I followed the group – the operators – outside onto a small loading dock overlooking a crowded parking lot. Somehow, navigating the various hallways around the Lowlife bar, we'd ended up on the other side of the block from where we'd parked.

With more light, I could finally see Vikk in his full glory: roughly seven feet of cybernetics wrapped in mottled brown Sevenex armor panels. The soft panels were arranged to look somewhat like human muscles, but thankfully, they made no such attempt with the head. Rather than looking like some grim, metal skull, Vikk's face was more of a big mannequin head with sensors and cameras.

Taking all that in, I was sure of one thing: compact cars were of no use to this group. I guess we'd be getting into a van or...

Katarina's eyes flashed and I heard the sound of direct-thrust engines spooling up from the far end of the parking lot. A cloud of dust and trash kicked up from that direction, drawing my eyes to a matte black Above-Road Vehicle the size of a small cargo truck. Six electric thrusters hummed along the sides of the angular ARV, and yellow lettering on the side spelled out "GREYSEN SECURITY".

"Uhhhh, company car?" I asked Katarina as we all headed that way.

"Perk of the job. Plus, it's hard for the big one here to travel in anything smaller," Katarina said, nodding toward Vikk. "*Possible*, but a real asspain."

"I don't come to public much," Vikk droned, a strange accent tinting his digitized words. "But to meet you, is good I come."

With no inflection or body language to pull from, I couldn't tell if that was a compliment or some bare statement of fact. I smiled and thanked the golem anyway.

The side hatch of the ARV slid open wide as we approached. I climbed aboard with the others, holding my hair down against the pulsing wind of the idling thrusters. I'd never seen the inside of a GreySec ARV – most people haven't – but it was about what I expected. Bare bones and colored battleship blue/gray from floorboards to ceiling. Padded seats lined the sides of the cargo area, with one large seat taking up most of the rear bulkhead. Forward of the sliding door, a small cockpit provided a single pilot with wraparound external view screens, flight controls, and a console of readouts and panels – Katarina took that seat, natch.

The rest of us dropped into the seats in the rear bay, with Vikk taking the large, padded golem throne at the back. My seat had a nifty storage bin underneath, so I stowed my SevenArms container full of MMK cartridges there for the time being.

Tandy was the only one of us who pulled the safety harness over her shoulders and buckled it at her waist. If I didn't know better, I'd think she looked a little more pale.

I watched Katarina push a few touchscreens, then felt the ARV thrust straight up like a HEMA lift before tilting off toward our destination. It was surprisingly quiet inside the bay. Quiet and strangely comfortable. I guess Z was right when he said GreySec put a lot of care into everything they manufactured.

"Autopilot running," Katarina said before swiveling the pilot's seat around to face the rest of us. "Six minutes out, air traffic willing."

I was about to say something to Tandy, but changed my mind when I saw her sitting with her eyes closed and her fists clenched around the safety harness.

"Isn't it hard to stay...low profile...with all this?" I asked Katarina instead.

"You'd think, wouldn't you?" Katarina replied. "But in a city where everything is tracked, surveilled, and logged, hiding is more difficult than most people think. I figured out a long time ago that it's better to operate in the open and cover your tracks than to try to stick to the shadows."

"Hiding in plain sight," I whispered, looking toward Tandy.

"Thanks to six years of service with the HMPD side of GreySec, I have full use of this ARV during my shifts," she continued. "As far as using it for unofficial business, I either come up with good cover stories or Pilky alters the data."

"Just like I modified the imagers up there," Pilky added, pointing to an array of lenses along the top of the bulkhead. "And the telemetrics. They only see Katarina, and our added weight isn't logged or transmitted back to the execs and bit counters."

"And as far as anyone seeing us on the street, people either love or hate GreySec," Katarina continued. "So bystanders might want to praise us...or they might want to shoot us. But they have no reason to ask questions, much less go tattling to my bosses."

She watched me for a minute, probably noticing that I kept looking at Tandy.

"She's okay," Katarina said. "Hey, Tan, can I tell Jack about your condition?"

Tandy nodded quickly without opening her eyes.

"She took a fall as a kid," Katarina explained. "Caused some issues with her neurocom. They had to put her in emergency surgery to repair some of the interface meshing."

"Ouch," I whispered to myself.

"They fixed her up, but a complication didn't show itself until she got older. You know how meshing is installed right after birth so the brain can develop with the neural interface in place?"

"Yeah, I know the basics," I nodded. "The pathways adapt to the mesh and vice versa. Makes the whole thing work."

"Well, there's a reason it's done that way. It's impossible to map that kind of hardware to a fully-formed human brain. But these docs had to patch up some of Tan's loose nodes by hand. And they got some wires crossed. So now, she has...ya know, abnormal physical reactions to certain things. Violence is the main trigger. But we figured out pretty quickly that accelerating in an ARV does it, too."

"Skitz," I said. "So it makes her sick? Or what...makes her freak out?"

"No, luv," Pilky shook his head. "Gives her orgasms, believe it or not. Imagine if some surgeon wired your bloody fight-or-flight response into your nethers. That's 'bout what happened."

Then Pilky leaned over to me and whispered: "And as cheeky as I thought that was when we found out, the novelty 'as worn off, and I full-on feel bad for her."

I didn't know what to say, so I was grateful when the ARV slowed and began to descend. Then I saw Tandy's face again and felt bad about being grateful.

"Feels like we're almost there, Tandy," I managed through a sympathetic smile.

She didn't reply, but she didn't look offended either. My best effort at work.

Katarina swiveled forward again and pressed a few commands just before I felt the ARV touch solid ground. The final lurch was punctuated with the loud thump and hiss of impact absorbers on the bottom of the hull.

Tandy let out a huge breath and unlatched her harness. Then Pilky took a small cylinder from his breast pocket, held it to his nose, and inhaled – some kind of chem, I figured.

"Fancy a snoot?" he said, tipping the cylinder toward me.

I waved it off graciously. Thanks to the Luckies, I was no stranger to biohacking or taking a few stims before a job, but I didn't think a shopping trip called for it.

Pilky shrugged and pocketed the container as we all piled out of the ARV. We'd touched down on an asphalt flattop just big enough for the vehicle. The plain, com-crete buildings all around didn't look familiar, but my nose knew where we were.

Airship fuel, street food, and filth.

"Smells like Camden Cay," I said, looking for more landmarks to be sure. "I was just here."

"Next to it. And you haven't been where we're going," Katarina said. "Come on."

"I stay," Vikk said flatly, crouching beside the ARV. "Is car insurance."

Everyone chuckled as we made our way down a nearby alley.

"You'll start to understand Vikk better the more you're around him," Tandy said, stepping beside me. "So much processing power goes into moving all that cyber around that his voice functions are basic as hell. But he actually cracks jokes more than anyone."

"Plus, that accent doesn't help," Pilky added. "Pan-Asian Coalition veteran and expat. From somewhere in Siberia, originally. Defected to the EU, then ended up here."

"Sounds like he could write one hell of a memoir," I said, then scratched my ear. "Wait...wasn't the PAC dissolved in like 2095?"

We crossed a lifeless street, and then cut down another alley between a matched pair of tall apartment buildings.

"Too right," Pilky said. "Vikk is an old boy. Eighty-three, or summat near it."

"Eighty-three years old?" I gasped. "No way. Golems don't work like that."

"That golem does," Pilky shrugged.

Our group turned through a shadowy courtyard in the middle of a tenement, then between two more identical, plain buildings.

"Alright, kiddos," Katarina cut in just as we stopped at the edge of a deep, com-crete-lined drainage canal. "Down we go."

"What is this zone? It's like a morgue. I haven't seen a single person since we got out of the ARV." I asked.

"Redevelopment zone on the east side of the Cay, about fifteen blocks square. No reason for anyone to be in here except druggos and opt-outs. But we have regular patrols for vagrancy or suspicious activity. I'm actually here to inspect and set new patrol orders right now."

"You mean as far as the logs go, right?" I asked.

Katarina grinned. "You're getting it."

"What is a 'redevelopment zone' anyway?"

"When part of a district gets too dirty, broken down, and lawless, it gets redeveloped. First, everyone is evicted and moved to city shelters or housing, depending. Then the whole zone gets cleaned up, rebuilt, and fixed as needed. Some former residents go back, and some get shuffled back into another district."

"That's skitz. Rounding people up like animals, just moving them away from their home"

"Honestly," said Katarina, "It's not the worst corporate protocol we have to enforce. The people get medical care during the transition and eventually get put into better zones – or even redistricted if they're really lucky. It also helps with crime, trafficking, and disease."

"How long does that take? Getting them into new homes?"

"Well, this has been an RDZ for two years," Katarina replied. "Initial cleanup is done, which is why you can actually see the roads and get between the buildings. I'm sure most of the former residents have been rehoused by now. But a few hundred will be on the waiting list to come back here once the redevelopment is finished."

I could already tell Katarina was going to be an interesting friend. Another person with one foot in the corpo world and one foot out here in the streets.

"Down here," she said, pointing to a steel ladder leading to the base of the drainage canal. "Drone flybys are rare here, but they do happen."

I climbed about nine feet down into the com-crete canal, followed by the rest of the crew. There was no water at the bottom, but a thick buildup of greenish sludge covered most of the floor.

It reminded me of a job I did with the Luckies during my first week as a bond. These drainage canals ran through the entire city, including the Quarters, so the Luckies used them to get around quietly inside their crap-heap of a district. That day, we'd used them to sneak up on a rival gang's drug lab.

This was different. Following Katarina and the crew down this canal felt a lot less like sneaking and more like strolling. Eventually, we got to a section of the canal covered by metal grating rather than open to the sky. Shortly after, she stopped at a thick service hatch clearly built to be watertight.

"I love this location," Katarina said. "I can fly in whenever I want. Everyone else can get here using the canals."

"I could live without the slime," Tandy added. "But it's better than trying to do this at street level."

"Do what?" I asked.

Instead of answering, Katarina threw open the metal hatch and gestured for me to step in. Beyond was a tube-shaped corridor well-lit by overhead LED bars. About twenty feet down, there was another hatch. I walked toward it as Katarina sealed up the entryway behind us.

Pilky, Tandy, and Katarina's footsteps echoed behind me. The second hatch popped open as I got closer. Noticing a MiFi receiver hidden on the wall next to it, I figured Katarina must have opened this one with a neurocom signal. Clever.

The door swung open completely revealing a huge dude with camo-dipped cyber arms and a shotgun resting on his shoulder.

"Whoa!" I said, throwing up my hands.

"Is that Kat and friends I see?" the man growled, making a not-subtle effort to stand in front of a stack of empty beer cans.

"Dammit, Bluto," Katarina scowled as she walked past me and through the hatch, "I told you not to call me that. It's 'Miss Guterres'. And when you're posted, you stay straight."

She kicked over the dozen beer cans that Bluto had stacked into an artful little pyramid.

"You want me to tell Paco you're not following the rules? I'll bet he'd love taking a 500-scrip infraction out of your ass."

"No, Miss," he replied, gritting his teeth in genuine concern.

"Guterres."

"No, Miss Guterres."

Katarina locked eyes with the man for a few more seconds, looking every bit like a cat with her claws out after someone just stepped on her tail. Then she turned on her heel, waving for the rest of us to follow.

A bend in the tubular corridor took us into a section built for defense. Alternating walls of sandbags would give defenders ample cover, and a few of the emplacements had pintle mounts welded to the floor, ready to receive mounted weapons like machine guns or grenade launchers.

Though I couldn't imagine wanting to fire off a grenade launcher in these close spaces. Probably just machine guns, then.

"Tight security," I mumbled as we weaved through the sandbag walls.

"Wait 'til you see the rest of this place," Tandy said, smiling.

Chapter Twenty

THE UNDERCROFT

K atarina called it 'the Undercroft'.

If Satan built a shopping mall inside a giant soup can, it would probably look like this.

At the end of the defensive corridor, Pilky excused himself to "have a flutter" – whatever that meant – and Tandy and Katarina gave me the tour.

Undercroft was a giant cylinder, something the size of a small apartment building, about twenty stories from top to bottom. The inside walls of the cylinder had been built out with catwalks and gantries, making it into a verticalized open-air shopping center – open-air except that it was all sealed up underground, that is.

Katarina said it was part of a building's foundation, like a big water-collection cistern. The entire thing had been secretly sealed up and built out with stairs and catwalks by funneling construction resources from the D13 zone redevelopment project.

Tandy and Katarina called out different points of interest as we walked. A cybernetics chop shop, multiple gunsmiths, a sword and knife fabricator, a wetgear doc – we'd be going back to that one, they said.

Natch, there were also a couple of bars, a tiny casino, a tattoo parlor, and a handful of street food carts on the bottom level.

"This is weird. Like a whole city block under a city block." I said, taking it all in.

"This," Katarina said, raising her arms and smiling, "is my Tortuga."

"What's a 'Tortuga'?"

"A pirate city. A *free* city. A place where the freebooters and privateers can come to conduct business with some order and protection."

"She really likes pirates," Tandy whispered without an ounce of judgment or derision.

"Five years I've been working to make a place like this," Katarina continued, "and here it is. I still get fraggin' glitches in my stomach every time I come down here."

"Wait, this is *your* place?" I asked. Somehow that part had been omitted from the tour.

"Mine and a few others that helped make it happen. Zoroaster was a big part. It was a group effort to manifest, but I will damn well take credit for the vision," Katarina smiled.

"This place makes mad scrip from taxing the vendors," Tandy winked. "And a few gangs work security and maintenance for the privilege of getting in the door."

"Like Bluto out there in the hallway?" I asked.

"Yeah, like that fragwit," Katarina groaned. "Proof that there are still some kinks to iron out in the protocol."

If Undercroft was bringing in the crypto, it would explain how Z and the crew had access to so much high-end gear. On top of that, Katarina's position at GreySec probably opened up all kinds of opportunities for getting everything from drugs to military-grade weapons.

It was all starting to make sense, at least from a logistics angle. But I was still having a hard time understanding where all the pieces fit together. I needed a chance to ask more questions without pushing my newbie status too far. Maybe Z himself would be the better one to ask.

"We gonna get this girl her new shine, or what?" Tandy said, pointing a thumb toward the wetgear docshop.

"Let's do it," Katarina said, gesturing for us to lead the way.

The inside of the docshop wasn't pristine, but it was brightly lit, clean, and orderly – all things you appreciate in a place that installs and fixes cybernetics. Inside was a wide open space except for what looked like a small office in the back. The main showroom in the front featured walls of hanging wetgear, everything from replacement hands to enhanced eyes in sealed sterile bags. Tandy was already poking through the selection.

A single MedBed sat in the center of the showroom, ready and waiting for a customer.

"Welcome! Welcome!" a man's voice with a gruff, latino edge bellowed from the back of the shop.

An overweight and heavily tattooed man lumbered out wearing a white tank top. His welcoming smile looked to be made entirely of gold.

"Tandy! And Miss Guterres! You bring me another new customer," he said, waddling over to shake my hand.

"So good to me!" he told me, maintaining too much eye contact. "*Gracias*, Miss Guterres."

"*De nada*, Ricardo," Katarina replied. "Keep paying your rent ahead, and I'll bring you all the customers you can handle."

She turned to me and continued the introduction.

"This is Jack. Jack, Doc Ricardo here is a newer tenant. He's only been here a month, but he paid a year in advance and doesn't make trouble."

"No! No trouble. Miss Guterres brought me here to get me out of trouble," the man laughed.

"Ricardo's old shop was in Santos territory, and he was getting behind with their protection payments. I caught on to his struggle through official channels after they shot up his store. Then I offered him a better protection deal," Katarina smiled.

"What happens if a Santos goon comes in here?" I asked.

"They don't know about us. And once they find out, we won't let them in. Better for business if we can keep the ganger custom down to a minimum. I prefer to keep it to mercs and freelancers."

"*Más* money and less bullshit, eh, girls!" the man laughed again. "So what can I get your new friend, eh?"

I shifted from foot to foot and scanned the merch along the walls, noticing that Tandy had moved on to browsing a holo catalog toward the back of the shop.

"I really wasn't planning on getting scalpelled today," I said, looking at Katarina. "Not that I'm against it..."

"No problem! No replacements yet anyway," Ricardo waved his hand. "Only upgrades. I do not have all the equipment yet for organ and limb removals. Soon though! Soon! You see my new bed, ah? One step closer."

"Well then, my arm and leg are pretty...outdated."

Katarina chimed in: "We're looking for durability. Graphene casing, Class III or better. Security Link on the hand, for sure. Something we can get a matched set for later."

Ricardo whipped an imaging visor out of his pocket and shook it. The long, narrow sensor package lit up green, and he gestured for me to pull up my sleeve.

"Ah, *sí, sí, sí,*" he mumbled while examining my wetgear arm, first with his eyes, then with his visor.

"It is old, chica, like me," he bellowed another laugh. "Prolly just as many...ehh...creaks and pains when it moves, too. Ha ha! *Ven acá,* up on the bed. Let me see the leg."

His visor showed him everything he needed to know right through my leggings.

"Good," he said, pocketing the visor. "Both BioDyne, generation *cuatro y seis*...ehhhh, the arm and leg. Different. But for both I have something backward compatible. BioDyne, gen *siete*. Best upgrades I can do with your existing mounts."

Ricardo walked over to the wall and pulled two large sealed bags down.

"Ah! I have cores your size," he smiled. "*Perfecto.* I can print casings in Kevlar or gyroid graphene. I do not have Sevenex for these models in stock."

"How about synthskin?" I asked.

"Ohhhh, ha ha! Very expensive! Not...ehh...robust. You want robust, *sí*?"

"Yeah, Ricardo," Katarina replied. "Graphene only. No synthskin. I'm not paying for that just so it can get ripped off the first time you get in a fight."

She gave me a flat look that reeked of judgment. As if I wasn't taking this seriously enough or something.

"Okay, Miss Guterres!" Ricardo continued while scanning the wall of parts. "Ehh...I need to swap out the hand...ah!"

He pulled down a much smaller bag and carried the whole lot over to the MedBed.

"BioDyne core, SevenArms processor, TaoCom interfaces. A real...ehhh...gunslinger's hand, *chica*! Bang bang!"

"I've never even held a gun with S-Link," I said.

"Duh," Tandy said without taking her eyes off the holo catalog, "if you had, you'd be missing a hand."

The doc laughed and nodded in agreement.

"That should be it for now," Katarina said. "Ricardo, get this all installed. And Jack, we'll bring you back for more when Ricardo is fully operational. Get you some eyes to go with the new hand."

Hm. But I like my eyes. I wonder if I'll have a say in these upgrades.

"*Sí*, miss. This should take..hmmm...two hours, the most."

"Roger that," said Katarina, heading for the door. "I'm going to do some rounds, check the tenants. Meet me at the gun stall on level two when you're done."

"I'll wait with Jack," Tandy called out.

The woman grunted acknowledgment and exited.

I watched the doc unsealing my new upgrades and looking each one over in turn. He looked more serious now, focused on his work. I was grateful for that.

"Ready to start, *chica*," he said, rolling over a standing tray of precision tools. "Take off the jacket and the leggings, *por favor*. You can leave the shirt."

I pulled them off and set them on a nearby counter.

"Ricardo, does Kat...Miss Guterres...bring a lot of people in for upgrades on her tab?" I asked, climbing back onto the MedBed.

Ricardo took a breath, but before he could answer, Tandy bounced over and gently patted his cheek.

"Now, now! The doc isn't supposed to talk about his patients. Right doc?" she smiled.

"Anyway, Jack...you should see some of the new wetgear in the catalog! I heard you say you wanted synthskin, but these new platinum finishes...mmm...so sick!"

Tandy continued raving over the new lineup pretty much the entire time Ricardo went to stripping apart my old arm and leg down to the mounts and installing the new gear in their places. His 3D printers had been running in the back room during the procedure, cranking out dissolvable molds for the graphene casings.

He told me about the procedure as he worked, explaining that the molds would be run through a graphene nanocoating machine that created hundreds of atom-thick layers in precise geometric forms called 'gyroids' – too small to see without imagers. After the layers hardened, the molds would be chemically dissolved, leaving contoured outer panels for my limbs that were hundreds of times stronger than steel and five times as bullet resistant as Kevlar.

"It's crazy that Sevenex is supposed to be better than this," I said, running my hand over the newly-installed casings. "This stuff is amazing. It weighs nothing and is so thin it can still look like a normal limb."

"Hmmm...Sevenex is not always better," Ricardo said, stepping back to admire his work. "Is flexible, but is also thick and heavy. *Muy* complex. Technology can fail...graphene, no. It is just tough."

I also knew that Sevenex had another weakness, which was why so many street toughs and gangers carried knives and swords along with their hot steel. The amazing tech was great at obliterating an incoming bullet, but nearly useless at stopping a sharp blade.

"You are all set, *chica*."

"Thanks, Ricardo," I said, extending my upgraded hand.

He shook it and flashed his row of gold teeth, obviously satisfied with his work.

"Yeah, thanks, Ricardo!" Tandy bubbled, grabbing my other hand to lead me out of the docshop.

Beyond the shop's sliding doors, Undercroft was still humming with activity. There had to be at least a hundred people wandering around, checking out the various goods and services. If they really were mostly mercs and lancers, it was more of them than I'd seen my whole life.

"Gun store!" Tandy smiled, still pulling me along. "Gun store, fun store! I'm excited, can you tell?"

Her condition made me wonder what kind of excitement we were talking about here.

"I can tell," I laughed. "How could I not?"

She stopped, and for a second, I worried that I'd hurt Tandy's feelings. She took my hand in both of hers and slid into a serious tone...relatively speaking.

"It's just, I don't get to go on any jobs with a lot of action," she said. "You know why. Now. Sometimes even *holding* a gun or a sword can make me...too excited. So that's why I'm usually on phantom duty, doing the boring counter-surveillance stuff."

"It's really that bad, huh?"

"It's awful," she sighed. "I hate it...but I also like it. But not really by choice. And I don't even know what my choice is because it's all the stupid bio-neural crap making it happen. That's the worst part. I don't even know which feelings are really mine."

"Like...if you get turned on, you never know if it's really *you* getting turned on?"

Tandy nodded.

"I can't even imagine what that's like," I shrugged, "but who cares, right? If you like something you like it. I've seen a lot worse crap in this city than someone who gets horny from holding a gun."

I gazed around the Undercroft, grinned, and leaned in to whisper: "Look at all these people. Mercs and gangers. I'm pretty sure all of them get off on gunfire. That's why they're here."

Tandy chuckled, then nodded a sort of half-agreement.

"Let's go," I said. "I'm sure Katarina is waiting for us. Or 'Miss Guterres'. What's with that, anyway?"

Chapter Twenty-One

FIREPOWER

Katarina watched as Tandy and I approached her at the gun seller's stall. The location was open in the front and held a row of folding tables down the center, each covered with polymer bins. Dozens of different firearms hung from the three surrounding walls.

"Let's see it," she said, nodding toward my arm.

I held my left palm up, showing her the S-Link connector plates designed to link up with certain types of weapons.

"Nice," Katarina grinned. "How do they feel?"

Hm. Tandy had pulled me out of the docshop so fast, I hadn't even thought about it. I moved my arm in a circle and balanced on the wetgear leg.

"Really good, actually. So good I didn't even notice. But smooth, responsive."

"And these can take a rifle bullet and keep ticking," said Katarina. "Speaking of..."

She reached behind the nearest table and pulled up a thin, black ballistic vest.

"This is yours, too. Gotta protect the guts. Much harder to replace, trust me."

She tossed it to me, and I turned it over in my hand. It was lightweight and soft, only a little thicker than a sweater. Definitely not the bulky armor I'd seen most people wearing.

"That's GreySec issue for covert ops," Katarina explained. "Light enough to wear under anything. It's made from good, old-fashioned nano-ceramic gel that will stop a knife or a bullet. But only once. Maybe twice if the hits are far enough apart."

"Stuff is liquid until something hits it, then it turns harder than steel," Tandy said. "And the gel absorbs most of the hit, so you don't feel it as much."

"You sure about that?" I asked.

"I was wearing one like this when I got shot in the back. Not on purpose; I was in a bad place when a gunfight kicked off," she smiled.

Such was life at street level in Hope Megacity, at least in the low-status districts.

"Put it on," Katarina said. "Under your jacket is fine. Might as well get used to shooting with it on."

"So, we're shooting next?" I asked, sliding off my jacket. "I'm down."

I didn't have a lot of gun practice to speak of. Apart from the few times I ended up using one with the Luckies, I'd only shot a few bottles in an alley. And that was only because some rando wanted an excuse to talk to me.

He stopped me on the street, said he wanted to buy me a drink. I pointed at his holstered automatic and said I'd rather try shooting. He took me up on it, but I don't think he realized the stupidity of putting a gun in the hands of the girl he was trying to skeeze on until I started blasting bottles.

That was a short date.

I donned my hooded jacket over the armor while taking a look at the selection. Assault rifles, shotguns, handguns – automatics and revolvers. Some pretty exotic stuff I didn't recognize. All available in colors ranging from blued steel to bright pink with leopard print accents.

"What am I looking for here?" I asked Katarina.

"Small and concealable. We're not airdropping you into Brazil. Think 'personal protection'."

I scanned the selection of pistols until my eyes landed on a strange-looking automatic. It was sort of like a regular handgun but with a longer slide, extended magazine, and a little fold-up foregrip in front of the trigger guard. Most notably, the whole thing was flat black with neon blue tiger stripes.

"Oh," I whispered. "Jack likes it."

"You'll have a hard time hiding that on your narrow-ass waist, but it'll fit in your bag for sure," Katarina said, smirking.

She waved to the vendor and pointed. The man walked over, pulled the weapon from the wall, and handed it to the woman.

"Gallardo automatic, PDW conversion with S-Link add-on," she said, looking the weapon over. "Caseless 10mm, 24-round magazine. Five-round burst mode. Not a bad pick, Jack."

She checked the chamber and handed the PDW – personal defense weapon – over to me.

"Hate the color though," she grinned.

"I like it," I smiled and aimed it toward the wall. "Feels good."

"You'll have to hold it in your left hand once we set up the S-Link. It doesn't have theft protection because it's a conversion, but it does have a user lockout."

Meaning it wouldn't fry an arm with electricity if it was picked up by an unregistered user, but it wouldn't fire, either.

"No problem," I said, switching my grip. It felt just as good in my left hand. Before bio-neural enhancement, most people had *one* dominant hand. Suckers.

"That's all the more reason to get that organic arm swapped out, though," Katarina added. "Stronger, faster, better. And we can set you up with more S-Link perks later. How'd you like to shoot around corners?"

What the hell did she – and Z – have planned for me? It seemed like I was getting a lot of attention and free upgrades for a newbie on the crew.

"Yeah, around corners. That's hot. Soon enough, right?" I said, forcing a grin.

I was definitely going to have a chat with Z when I got back to the bunker.

"Put it on my tab," Katarina said to the vendor.

She grabbed a few spare magazines from one of the composite bins nearby, along with a box of ammo. "And these."

The vendor nodded and walked to his terminal to punch in the details.

Katarina turned to me and said: "We have a firing range on the third…"

A neurocom notification in my head pulled my attention. An incoming voice message.

It was Alice. I played it.

"Jack," her voice came through. "We need to talk. Meet me in the atrium of my building. I'll wait there until sunrise."

She sounded…scared? I wasn't so sure.

"Please come," the message continued, then the notification disappeared from my NUI.

"Hey," Katarina said. "What's going on?"

I stammered, and almost turned around to run for the exit. Then I tried to hand the Gallardo back to Katarina. She pushed it back to me, so I mindlessly stuffed it in my backpack next to Bugger.

"You okay?" Tandy asked.

"I think...I think I need to go. Someone commed," I said.

"Whoa there," Katarina said. "Slow down. You need backup or what?"

I shook my head and turned to run, but Tandy grabbed my arm.

I couldn't say anything. My tongue was frozen. But I saw Katarina wave her hand as if to say 'let her go'. Tandy complied, and I rushed toward the exit.

A million questions flooded my mind. What happened to Alice? Did they find out that I contacted her? Was she in trouble?

When I reached the hatch, I looked back and saw Katarina still staring at me, her eyes flashing green.

She was comming someone, most definitely. I didn't have time to worry about who.

Chapter Twenty-Two

Once out of the Undercroft, I navigated through the redevelopment zone using the drainage canals. Back at street level, it was only a twenty-minute metro ride to get to Alice's building.

It was definitely the longest twenty minutes of my life.

I tried to maintain some level of vigilance while running up the steps to the HEMA-7 atrium – the word "professional" still kicking around in my head. Scanning my surroundings, I saw the usual crowds and vendors, and street food trash blowing in the breeze. Nothing looked out of sorts.

It took a bit of searching to find Alice in the midst of it all, but I finally spotted her sitting at the same table near the vending machines that I'd sat at a few days earlier. I ran to her, my backpack bouncing against me, the new addition of hot steel banging into my kidney.

"Allie!" I said, looking around one last time before sitting across from her.

"Jack! You came. Thank you…"

She looked half as put together as she had a few days ago, and twice as surprised to see me.

"...I thought maybe they'd already gotten to you," she added, her face pensive.

"What? Of course I came. *Who* would have gotten to me?"

"TaoCom," she whispered, her eyes darting from face to face in the mulling crowd. "Their security teams, or mercs. I don't know who they are."

"What?" I flashed a reassuring grin. "I saw the security bulletin. I know they made me. But it's okay..."

"No!" Allie cut in, her eyes filling with tears. "Not the bulletin. The...I don't know. They came to my apartment. Asked questions about you. If I'd seen you. If I knew anything about you. What did you do, Jack?"

I cocked my head back, recoiling from the accusation.

"What did *I* do? How about your corpo buddies, sending out hit squads? They're the ones who knocked on your door!"

Tears rolled down her cheeks.

"You knocked first, Jack," she said, choking back a sob.

"So, why did you need me?" I asked, tempering my emotions. "Are you in trouble? Did they threaten you?"

"I don't know," she whispered. "I wanted to tell you. But I don't know how to help you. And now they're..."

She froze, her eyes locked on something behind me.

I turned quickly, but not quick enough to avoid the hand grabbing my shoulder. A hooded face in shadow pulled in close to mine.

"Jack," he said. "We need to go. Now!"

I recognized the voice, and fear melted back into confusion.

"Mallus? What the hell?"

"You're compromised," he said, pulling back his hood. "Three hostiles. Maybe more. They watched you come in, and now they're on the move."

I looked to Allie, eyes wide and holding back panic, then back to Mallus. He let go of my shoulder, standing tall to scan over the crowd.

"Skitz, Allie," I asked, burning a look into her panic-stricken eyes. "Did you do this? DID YOU?"

She couldn't hold back after that. Alice broke down into tears, her whole body shaking as she buried her face in her crossed arms. All at once, I felt my heart breaking and my adrenaline surging.

"We go, or we get flatlined," Mallus said. "C'mon!"

Not much of a choice, so I jumped to my feet. Mallus led the way toward the back of the atrium, clearing a path through the foot traffic with his shoulder. Alice stayed behind, still crying. I didn't know what to make of it, but there was no time to wonder about leaving her.

"Car's this way," he said, voice shaking.

We hit an exit door, and he shoved it open at a run. Once out on the sidewalk, he pulled a hefty, red revolver from under his hoodie. I took the cue and drew my new Gallardo from my bag. Actually, it was more like I fumbled it out backwards. My raced, and so did my thoughts.

I didn't see anything or anyone 'hostile', but Mallus was sure they were coming.

I followed him down the sidewalk, scanning for threats. The Edison came into view, purple in the street lights, about half a block down. The doors slid open, and I pumped my legs harder to close the distance.

A shot rang out. Then two more came so close to my head that my ear was ringing. Asphalt chips and dust exploded in front of me, and I dove behind a news kiosk. The Edison was so close...

Panicking, my eyes fell on Mallus. He'd taken cover near the car and was leaning out from behind a com-crete bench. After taking a few careful peeks, he fired his revolver twice at whoever was chasing us.

More bullets came our way in reply. A lot more.

I steadied my hand and leaned out with the Gallardo. There were at least five gunslingers coming for us, alternating between ripping off rounds and sprinting to reach us. I aimed the pistol, squeezed the trigger, and...

...click.

Then it hit me. No fragging bullets, Jack! I was in such a hurry to rush to Allie that I didn't grab them, and now I was gonna get my fragging head blown off.

Growling, I shoved the weapon back into my bag. Doing a real bang-up job on the professional thing so far.

"Jack!" Mallus yelled. "Get in the car!"

"You kidding, man?" I yelled back, gesturing to the air that was filled with flying lead.

He held up a frag grenade and shook it.

"Run. To. The. Car. NOW!" he yelled, pulling the pin.

The grenade soared out of his hand in slow motion, spiraling past me as I launched to my feet. I was almost at a full sprint when the grenade detonated, and by the time I jumped into the Edison's passenger seat, the sounds of gunfire had died down.

I peered over the dashboard, looking for Mallus. He was on his feet, grinning at the smoking hole he'd put in the sidewalk.

He turned to run to the car, then a cloud of red mist exploded from his arm. His revolver, and the hand that was holding it, dropped to the ground at his feet. Mallus' grin disappeared, and he fell forward into a growing puddle of blood.

I froze. I thought about running to help him, but my feet wouldn't move. Two of the hostiles surrounded him and the feeling of slow motion kicked in again. Time slowed, as if my heartbeat was going so fast that reality couldn't keep up.

One of the bastards kicked him in the head, sending him to the ground. The other stepped on his back.

My NUI flashed a notification, just as I realized two more were still moving toward me. It was Mallus, transferring the Edison's driver registration to my neurocom. He followed it with a one-word text message:

Run.

I shifted to the driver's seat and started the car with a MiFi signal. The doors slid shut and the electric motors hummed. Slamming my foot into the accelerator sent the car a block down the street before I could take my next breath.

"Skitz, where the hell do I go now?" I mumbled to myself, trying to find a good route away from the mess.

I could hear HMPD sirens coming from ahead, but that wasn't what had me freaking. It was the sound of motorcycles closing behind the Edison. Loud, deep. Not like the screaming street bikes that the Japanese gangers loved, and definitely not electric.

Nah, I was being followed by the obnoxious exhaust sounds of chromed, ape-hanging road cruisers.

The Luckies. But it couldn't be them, right?

Activating the rearview camera in my NUI confirmed it. A swarm of leather-clad goons on cruisers closed fast. Ten, maybe more. The kill code had been nasty, but it clearly didn't have the city-wide reach Goodwin had bragged about when he pawned it off on me.

I wanted to punch the throttle again, but thickening traffic ahead made it impossible. It wasn't gridlocked, but it was close. Weaving through what I could, I pulled up a traffic display on MegaMaps and looked for the clearest route. Destination unknown – all I cared about was getting some distance.

The map sent me down a side street, and the Edison took the corner like a champ. The bikes had no trouble following, though; they definitely had the advantage at maneuvering between cars.

A sharp right, then back on a six-lane straightaway – the elevated express cutting from Quadreca to the Quarters, my old digs. No one wanted to go there, so the traffic was light as promised. I kicked the accelerator to the floor.

The Edison was a damn fast car, but the bikes weren't letting up. The lidar readout on the rearview camera made sure I was aware of it. 200 meters. 100 meters. 50 meters...

The bikes' engines roared so loud, I didn't need a readout to tell me one was pulling right up beside me on my left. Then more on the right. A front wheel came into view right outside my window. Then handlebars, gripped by flexing arms covered in tattoos. Then...that face.

A face that looked like it had melted in the sun. Drooping lip, sagging eyes. Just like he looked in the dream.

Monk. His face was ruined, but that didn't make it any harder to read his intentions. He was pissed. Too pissed for a dead guy.

Just as I thought to jerk the wheel and send the bastard flying off his loud-ass bike, he braked hard and got behind the Edison. I was so busy watching him, I didn't notice his buddies on my right were getting ready to take a shot at my head.

The deafening roar of a shotgun blast and a shower of broken glass gave that away. I laid on the brakes out of reflex, nearly taking the car sideways before recovering. Wind rushed in from the busted side window, and the car became a full-on echo chamber of exhaust notes and laughing goons. Beyond the guardrails on either side, the city continued to speed by.

Another shot rang out, this time hitting metal.

"Just don't hit the tires," I whispered. "Ohhhh...please don't."

That they hadn't just shot out one of my tires made me think they wanted to take me alive. Or at least they wanted to make a solid go at it. Hard to do if they rolled the car and turned me into a 100 mile-an-hour smear on the pavement.

That meant I just had to keep going. I'd be good until they got bored, at least.

A bike came up on the right again. Ducking low, I waited for another spread of buckshot. Not so lucky. This time, the rider grabbed the passenger door and launched himself halfway through the busted window.

Damn, I forgot. They get bored *fast*.

The son of a bitch laughed as he pulled himself in, flashing a row of yellow teeth under a glowing cybernetic visor implant.

"Got you, you little bitch!" he growled, reaching a black wetgear arm toward me.

I reacted, snatched my MMK from the sheath on my belt, and swung it hard at the Luckies' head. The blade sliced through his cheek, and I followed the spray of blood onto the windshield just in time to see a car coming up ahead. I swerved to avoid it, and the intruder had to stop groping at me long enough to steady himself.

That gave me the chance to draw back the knife and jab it straight into his temple. The black arm went limp instantly. Gravity and high speeds did the rest, pulling the Luckies' body from the car, leaving nothing but a dark pool of blood in the seat beside me.

A small win, but glancing ahead, it looked like it would be the only one. There were stopped cars and com-crete barriers snarling up the skyway a half mile ahead. Damn… I forgot about the checkpoint to enter the Quarters.

I had to slow down. Even though there were HMPD badges at the checkpoint, I'd be dead before they could do anything to help me.

Engines revved, and victorious laughter erupted all around me as the Luckies realized their prey was about to be cornered.

Then came the distinct whistling sound of directed-thrust motors.

A black ARV rose skyward from behind the guardrail to my left. The thruster-powered vehicle listed sideways and dropped a huge, angry-looking cybergolem onto the street between me and the traffic jam before zipping off out of sight.

"Oh, Vikk…you are so my fragging hero right now," I cheered, not that anyone could hear it over the cacophony of yells and gunshots that rose up from every direction.

At least none of it seemed to be directed at me anymore.

I rolled to a stop and watched little puffs of carbon smoke erupt from Vik's armor as the Luckies' bullets and buckshot hit Sevenex and vaporized. The golem didn't so much as flinch at the incoming fire; he just slowly turned his head, surveying his targets.

My neurocom chimed an incoming call from Vikk.

"Stay in car," he droned, then disconnected.

The Luckies were off their bikes, walking slowly toward the golem, each one alternating between frantically emptying their weapons into him and reloading. I counted seven to one in this fight, but it didn't take an overclocked brain to know how it was going to turn out.

Vikk pointed his fists toward the gangers, unleashing an invisible fan of flechette rounds from his knuckles. All seven goons stopped in their tracks, then fell to the ground. He'd pierced a fatal and unprotected weak point on each one of them with a six-inch ferrous spike fired from an electromagnetic driver.

"Golem tech," I marveled. "The things you can do with a massive form factor."

Vikk lowered his arms, heading my way. I climbed out of the Edison – what was left of it – grabbed my bag from the backseat, and met him halfway. That put us right in the middle of seven dead Luckies – Camden chapter goons, from the patches on their leathers. And none of them looked like Monk.

But that was just another inexplicable problem that would have to wait.

"That was beyond shiny," I told Vikk. "Thanks for saving my ass. But Mallus is back there and…"

"We know," Vikk cut in.

"Are we gonna get him?"

"Is too late," the golem droned, and my heart sank.

I wanted to say something, but there wasn't anything to say that could matter at that moment.

"You make a mistake, Jack. Others…not happy."

No skitz. I grabbed my hair and pulled hard enough to keep everything that just happened from completely catching up to me. I was still standing in the middle of a bunch of dead Luckies. Monk was not only alive, but after me. Mallus was gone. And Alice…

At least Allie might *not* have set me up. If it had been corpo mercs chasing me, sure. But she wouldn't have turned me over to a bunch of goons.

Not Alice.

Chapter Twenty-Three

THE ARV

After Katarina swung the ARV around for an unceremonious pickup, she set course for Z's garage with only myself and Vikk in the cabin.

"We need to get you back underground, and I need to stay away from Undercroft," she said. "After you left, the police LionEye net started lighting up. You got pinged somehow."

The woman shot me a blatantly dissatisfied look. "If I hadn't told Mallus to shadow you, you'd be dead. Make no mistakes, you fragged up, Jack."

I slouched in the padded jumpseat. How could running to help one friend cause this much trouble?

"What happened to him?" I asked.

Katarina sighed.

"I don't know yet," she said. "We couldn't find him near the HEMA, just a lot of his blood. The goons might have taken him. HMPD definitely didn't. And he wouldn't *let* corpos take him if they showed up."

She punched a few commands into her terminals, and the ARV slowed, easing toward the ground.

"Pilky stayed at Undercroft to monitor the comm traffic. We have a full NetOps suite down there," Katarina explained as the vehicle landed with a hiss of impact absorbers. "Tan stayed with him to watch over the place."

The ARV shut down, and the side door slid open. I grabbed my bag and followed Katarina onto a large landing pad.

"Is Vikk coming?" I asked.

Katarina barely shook her head 'no'. I guess he often waited with the ARV a lot to avoid problems with onlookers...and low ceilings.

The landing spot looked fairly barren and unused. Two more GreySec ARVs sat quietly on the marked asphalt – one of them appearing long dormant and dusted with grime, the other half-covered with a green tarp that flapped in the breeze.

A ten-foot com-crete wall surrounded the whole lot, cracking with age and topped with coils of razor wire. We walked toward the only feature in the wall, a heavy security door with a sign reading 'SECURE ALL WEAPONS AND ARMOR'.

Katarina's eyes flashed, and the door's panel buzzed, then lit up red.

"Always with this door," she mumbled, pulling a GreySec ID batch from her body armor and tapping it against the panel.

The lights flicked to green, and the door popped open.

We exited onto a street, clearly in Z's neighborhood of Edgerun. Quiet, low-traffic, and mostly light industrial.

"GreySec substation," Katarina said, tilting her had back the way we'd come. "Used to lease it to the HMPD. Now it's just some forgotten blip in a database. But I can park there without raising questions."

We walked across the street and wound our way between a few buildings. It was less than a hundred meters from the substation to the garage.

"Convenient," I mumbled as we entered Z's garage.

"Not an accident," said Katarina. "Years of planning, just like Undercroft. Just like our whole network. Which is why we can't afford to have girls running off like fragwits and putting unnecessary risk on my lap."

The remark was equal parts cold and angry but delivered so matter-of-factly that it made me feel like a chungus for infinite reasons. Katarina opened the red door to the spiral stairs, and I wondered how badly Zoroaster was going to flame me.

She followed me in silence, down the steps, through the sally port full of books, and into the NetOps room. Z wasn't there.

Katarina leaned against a rack of hardware, her eyes flickering green. She was probably on neurocom with Pilky, or deep in her NUI trying to get more information through MetaNet news. I sat down in the NetOps chair – my usual place – a good enough spot to receive a verbal thrashing.

A few minutes later, Katarina returned her attention to the room – to me – and asked if I'd managed to save my new hot steel or if I'd lost it along with destroying the car.

I showed her the Gallardo in my backpack but didn't mention that I ran off without ammunition. She probably knew anyway.

The worst part was her tone and the way she looked at me. It's not like she and I had a long history, but to see someone go from one setting to another like that...

Had I triggered some kind of permanent mood shift in the woman?

A moment later, a loud clunk echoed through the NetOps room. An innocuous section of wall swung open, revealing another hidden passage that made me wonder how big this bunker actually was.

Zoroaster stepped out with his trademark duster draped over a skintight NetOps suit. "Jack, Jack, Jack," he muttered, walking to me and sitting on his rolling stool.

"I'm sure Katarina already debriefed you on how bad you screwed up out there," he said, his serious eyes revealing nothing about his feelings on the matter.

"We don't have time to waste going over that," he continued. "Things are in motion. The best I can figure, the shootout was just bad luck in regard to timing. The real threat is that both TaoCom and HighCastle have bounties on you as of this morning, complete with a kill-on-sight order for anyone harboring you."

I clenched my jaw, dropping my eyes to the floor. Allie wasn't lying. If those mercs *had* figured out that she was helping me, they prolly would have zeroed her right there in her apartment.

"As far as corporate bounties go, that isn't surprising for someone they consider a high threat. It was strange that they would consider you such a threat, though. Kind of baffling...until my data mining started yielding answers."

"Like what? What could make me a threat to two of the biggest GCs in the fragging world?" I asked.

"Simple answer is this new connection to BeanStalk," Z answered. "But also the data that you've already accessed. It took time to make any sense of the intel pulled from your brain partition, but it's...beyond valuable.

"Secret development projects, executive com logs. But we think the reason you're being hunted is this...."

Z held up a slate and activated the holoprojector. A 3D rendering of Hope Mega appeared, complete with the Skypillars and the web-like interconnections between them that formed HighHold, the city in the clouds. The rendering zoomed into a building somewhere near street level, added a connection traveling up through the middle of Promenade, and then ended in some sort of chair in TaoCom Skypillar right around cloud level.

"This," Z said through a smug smirk, "is a way to get into HighHold. Digitized human transportation."

"Holy hell, like a teleporter?" I said.

"More like the most complex 3D printing and engram mapping system ever devised," Z said. "We're talking about a mix of technologies that we had no idea existed at the level we see here."

"And they know you have this intel," Katarina added. "It's obvious because they're shoring up defenses. The whole sub-cloudline section of the TaoCom pillar is on lockdown. GreySec even put out alerts a few hours ago. Declared the airspace around it a temporary no-fly zone."

"So far, they're just hedging their bets," Z said. "They have no idea what you really know and how you would use the information. That gives us a head start. As long as we move fast, we can work their tech in our favor."

Z explained how the teleportation system worked. At the point of origin, the traveler is bio-imaged, and their engrams are mapped and digitized with a neural scanner. The digitized human is then transmitted to the destination, 3D printed, and medically revived – a perfect copy.

"The scanning and digitizing isn't the impressive part. The engram scanning is just an overclocked version of the same tech corporations use to prevent employs from smuggling data into and out of their facilities.

"What's bleeding-edge is how they're recreating a living human being at the destination. This involves an extremely complex 3D printer able to produce exact biological copies, including any integrated wetgear, all the way down to the atomic level. Neural activity, memories, everything."

"I think I get where you're going with this," I said. "As long as you can recreate their imaging tech to send someone through, you can use TaoCom's printer at the destination."

"Exactly! And Eli is already working on building that point-of-origin system. We've identified the ideal target printer on their network," Z said. "But here's the rub. We need *you* to go. Your unique ability to perceive the BeanStalk means that you are somehow – neurologically or technologically – connected to it."

"Great. Is this why you've been sheltering me...and upgrading me?"

"Based on early assessments of the data, I suspected something like this would come up, yes."

"So what happens to the version of me down here? The original?"

Zoroaster sighed and leaned back on the stool.

"This amped-up engram mapping process cannibalizes the brain," he said. "You'll leave a body behind, but that's all. A shell. The Tao-Com prototypes are designed to dissociate and recycle the remains for future print jobs. Our point-of-origin scanner will be less elegant by necessity."

"No way," I said, halfheartedly laughing off the idea. "Fragging nil, guys. I know I screwed up, but you're basically saying you want me to scramble my brain on a hunch. There's no way you know this is gonna work!"

"Look, Jack," Katarina said, moving to stand over me. "We can't make you go. But I can insist very strongly that you do. The way I see it, you owe me for a lost operator and a lot of coverup work."

"Hold up, Captain," Z said, raising his palm to Katarina. "I'm not going to force Jack – or anyone else – to do this."

Phew.

Z took a deep breath, then beamed a smile. "Jack, I just want you to hear me out. Listen to the mission parameters we've put together.

When you see what it means for you and your father, I think you'll reconsider."

Chapter Twenty-Four

THE MISSION

Zoroaster was fully against exploiting people, or so he told me. Part of a professional operation, he said, was fair compensation.

And if I 'volunteered' for this BeanStalk job, I would be compensated more than fairly.

"I'm offering you a complete buyout of your father's servitude contract," Z said. "Orchestrated through Eli's corporation. Western Nano buys it out, and your father walks."

Last I checked, that would be over half a mil in hard crypto, depending on the coin and the market. It had been my goal to pay that off for well over a year, and I was so far unable to put together a plan to get even a fraction of that scrip in my hands.

"On top of that, there's something even more personal on the table," the psycher continued. "I'm convinced that our objective in this operation will tell us everything we need to know about your puck implant and why you're able to see the BeanStalk."

"What, you want me to kidnap someone in HighHold? Some corpo know-it-all?"

"Nothing so risky," Z replied. "We're not going to HighHold. If anything, that's probably what they fear the most. Which means they're preparing for it. We're aiming for a lab in TaoCom Skypiller, presumably where the transporter technology was being developed."

"Katarina just said the Skypillar is on lockdown," I said. "Wouldn't that be the worst place to send me?"

"The entrances are locked down, yes. And the aerial approaches. But these diagrams show a lab on floor 223 of the pillar, just below cloud level."

"So the experimental prototypes are still there," I said. "And hopefully functional. Not mothballed?"

"Deactivated, but still connected to the BeanStalk. We just need someone to get into that lab and restart the transporter system. Once it's online, we can transmit you right into the heart of TaoCom's research center."

"So you have someone working on the inside?"

Zoroaster scratched a rough sideburn as if thinking how to answer.

"No, but you do," Katarina said. "A level-four researcher with sufficient clearance."

I arched an eyebrow. "You can't be serious. You had me going along with this, but that's just not gonna happen. I mean…I'm not putting Allie in that kind of danger. And she would never do it anyway…"

"Jack, we did some digging after you pulled that stunt. Did she tell you *why* she was questioned by corpo mercs?" asked Z.

"It wasn't because they knew you'd contacted her, which means you were at least smart enough not to call her on the TaoCom network," Katarina cut in. "They questioned her because she has racked up a shitload of debt. That makes her a 'workable asset'. Someone who is so desperate for a way out, they can be turned against their corporation. And they thought maybe you'd tried."

"But *you're* the one who's going to try, am I right?" I asked.

"We're very good at helping people like Alice," Z continued. "Getting them safe and out of their corporation's crosshairs. Erasing the debt."

"I thought you were against exploitation, Z?" I said with more than a little anger building in my voice.

"It's all about perspective, Jack. We're not asking her to give up anything that she hasn't already lost. Her future is dwindling at TaoCom. Debt and suspicion are enough to sour her chances of moving up. She'll probably get Disemploy status once they find some ambitious ladder-climber to replace her. And if they flag her as a risk, no other corporation will touch her."

It was a convincing argument, but I couldn't get past one thing: Allie shouldn't have her future decided by a bunch of strangers in a weird bunker. For all I knew, she was working out her problems on her own. Hell, Z and Katarina might even be making it all up.

"No," I said. "I'm not going to recruit her. And I'm not doing this if she's the one who has to flip the switch."

Z's face never changed. I returned the most resolute stare possible.

"Understood," he said, finally. "Katarina, get topside and start working on our other assets. Anyone who can get even remotely close to that lab. We have two days to pull this off, max, so don't spare the carrot or the stick."

"I'm on it," the woman said, her frustration lingering as she exited through the sally port. I waited to hear the exterior hatch slam shut.

"Thanks, Z," I said, letting out a sigh of relief.

"You're not making this easy on me," he grinned. "But in defending your friend, you *did* say that you're up for doing this."

For my father. If he ever had a chance of having a normal life again, it was this one.

"I guess I did," I sighed. "But now that I think about it, you never said how I'm supposed to get back. If you're only building the origin scanner and not the printer, I'm stuck up there, right?"

Zoroaster flashed his too-white teeth and clapped his hands together.

"This is where I'm going to need you to stretch your faith in me just a little bit further..."

Chapter Twenty-Five

INTO THE BEANSTALK

"About twenty minutes out, guys," Tandy called out from the front seat of our super-secret tactical vehicle.

The rusty cargo van was fitting ride for this operation. A shady, windowless van was where my journey with the crew began, and now we were coming full circle.

The difference was that this vehicle wasn't stripped bare on the inside. Thanks to all of the hardware Eli had installed in the cargo area, it had to be nearly scraping the asphalt. The three of us — myself, Eli, and Zoroaster — crammed into the back didn't help.

The New Texas CEO built his version of the transporter tech right into the back using a NetOps chair as the foundation. That's where I was strapped down, with huge packages of imaging hardware hanging over me from improvised mounts.

Every time the van hit a bump in the road, the entire thing shifted and creaked over me. At least nothing was sparking or smoking.

"I really hope this doesn't cook my brain," I said as Eli and Zoroaster rattled off numbers and passed a slate back and forth.

This was officially the first time I'd seen Z go anywhere but the bunker. Too bad we were all packed so tight that he was practically on top of me.

"You'll be fine," Eli smiled without taking his eyes off of the pigtail of cables he was fiddling with.

We were on our way to Corpo Promenade, which Z decided was the best place to piggyback onto the BeanStalk signal stream. He wanted to park the van right on top of the Hope Consortium medallion, literally in the middle of the BeanStalk, but Katarina reminded him that even with her help, the van would be ripped apart by machine gun fire before it even got close.

The best she could do was make sure the van had clearance for street parking within sight of the BeanStalk. She would also stop her GreySec underlings from searching the van and discovering this little circus.

"I still don't understand why you're helping," I said to Eli.

He shrugged, bobbing his head, too wrapped up in checking his imaging scanners to formulate his response.

A few moments later, as if remembering the question, he ventured an answer.

"Not all corporations are bad, and neither are all executives," he said after a time. "Commerce, capitalism, technological progress. Two hundred years ago, these were pretty much economic and social ideas. It's when they turned into a means to power that they started to go rotten."

"Interesting theory," I said.

"Trust me," Eli laughed, "anything you can think of turns rotten when you start to bring the social hierarchy into it. Folks who don't have power will do anything to get it, and folks who have power will do even more to keep it."

"And which one are you?" I asked him, grinning.

He smiled and forced his New Texas accent into overdrive: "Well, darlin', I'm just a cowpoke born about two-hundred years after he was 'sposed to be!"

Then he held up the slate and waved it over me. "I'm also the one holding the switch to this contraption, little lady, so you just better mind your manners," he winked, and I couldn't help but laugh in spite of myself.

"You chungs all grab-assin' back there. Making me jealous," Tandy added.

She'd made it very clear that driving was not her favorite job, but with Mallus still...unaccounted for...she had to step up. I tried not to think about it. There'd be time to look for him later.

Though I didn't know *how much* later. The most insane detail of this plan – as if the birds-eye view wasn't bad enough – was how I was supposed to get out of TaoCom Skypillar after I'd secured the objective.

Because the crew didn't have enough time to build their version of the most complex 3D printer in the world, I was supposed to transmit myself back out of the TaoCom lab and into...storage. Like a Jack backup. My bio-images and mental engrams would be stored in a brainer until Eli could put together a working destination printer.

He assured me it would take a week, tops.

I said 'hell-no-absolutely-not,' but then remembered that I was doing this for my father. And I was convinced through Z's kung fu skills with logic that going into storage was absolutely no different for me than going directly into a printer. Raw data doesn't experience the passage of time, he'd said.

"Sec," Z said, holding an index finger up to Eli.

His eyes flashed, and he stared off to the side for a moment before relaying to us that Katarina had finished briefing her patrol officers. Pilky, who was watching comms and DarkNet traffic from his setup in Undercroft, had also checked in and reported everything quiet so far.

Sadly, my favorite cybergolem didn't slot in on this job. Vikk wasn't the best choice for covert ops, and he most certainly wouldn't fit in the van, so he stayed behind to 'make sure Pilky do not screw it up, his job' – in his words.

Another flat delivery from the golem, but the more I got used to the weird combination of accent, digitizing, and humor, the more his jokes started to come across as damn near poetic, like some new form of post-apocalyptic, computerized haiku.

Meh, a limerick, at least.

"We're still waiting on the asset to infiltrate the lab and activate the destination transporter," Z said.

He was referring to the asset that Katarina 'secured' after I refused to coerce Allie into activating the TaoCom transporter.

Paying off TaoCom employs on the inside was a drop in the operational expense bucket. After all the palm greasing, record spoofing, fabrication, and the cost of freeing my father, we had to be running up a tab in the high six figures.

And Z wasn't even slightly hesitant about it. That's how sure he was that the objective – the TaoCom research department's data center – was going to pay off.

That was my target. I had to make my way from the lab to a secure terminal in a nearby room and fix a wireless commlink to the research department's air-gapped storage drives. With that, Pilky would hack his way into the data, but I would still have to transfer it to the storage partition in my brain and bring it home.

Apparently, TaoCom didn't mess around when it came to data exfiltration protection, Their encryptions were designed to shred the files if they were subjected to any wireless transfer protocol.

"We're close, boys," Tandy said. "I see the piggy checkpoint up there."

Eli and Z looked at each other and nodded. I guess they were ready, but the closer we got to the Promenade, the more my anxiety crept in.

"They should wave you through, Tandy," Z said. "And point you right to our parking spot. I want to be ready to fire this thing up the second you stop."

"I'm picking up the data stream, big man," Eli said, tapping away at his slate. "Just like you said. I'm linked into Jack's neurocom feed, and however she's picking it up, it's carrying over to our transmitters."

Z's eyes flashed. He nodded his head and smirked. "The transporter prototype just came online."

"We're through the checkpoint," Tandy called back.

"Get ready, Jack," Eli smiled down at me. "Almost time."

I took a deep breath and closed my eyes. Seizing a rare opportunity to play 'the dying girl who wanted to know the truth', I steeled myself to ask a hard question.

"I have something I need to ask you before I go," I said to Z.

"Go for it, Jack."

"Did you write the kill code that started all this?"

Zoroaster hesitated for a moment, then nodded, "Yes."

"And did you give it to Goodwin to give it to me?"

"No, Jack. That I promise you. That kill code was never meant for you or anyone close to you. Goodwin stole it from me. Along with many other things."

"I feel like that might be a story we don't have time for right now," I said flatly.

"Very right," Z grinned. "But we will soon. I'll explain everything."

The van rocked to a stop, and Tandy turned in her seat, her eyes sparkling with excitement. "Clear!"

Eli pressed a button and everything went dark.

THE LAB

Why did my chest hurt? And my stomach...

Oh hell...when was the last time I ate? I've never been this hungry...

My eyes snapped open. Pretty dark in here. Was I in a fragging coffin? Something felt very wrong.

My neurocom. It wasn't booting – or at least the NUI wasn't working. I couldn't see any notifications. No logs. No signals. Was this the first time I'd ever woken up without seeing it? Yeah, for sure it was.

Oh frag, the transporter! It must have worked, and I must have been inside the destination printer! That's what this big tube thing was around me.

"How do I get this stupid thing open?" I mumbled.

I felt for a panel or a latch. Nothing. I banged my fists against the paneling.

Then the door swung open, but not because I hit it. Because the person standing outside opened it. Light flooded in, and my eyes struggled to make out the face.

"Jack," she said, and it felt like a foggy memory playing back.

Maybe I was dreaming again.

"Are you okay, Jack?"

I squinted and rubbed my eyes. Some focus came back, slowly. Shadows turned into objects. The silhouette of a short woman turning into a familiar sight.

"Allie?" I asked, rubbing my eyes again. "You aren't supposed to be here."

"Yeah, Jack, it's me. C'mon," she said, grabbing my wrists and pulling me out of the tube.

"No, really, you aren't supposed to be here. I told them not to make you do it."

I patted myself all over checking for missing body parts or gear. Knife, pocket interfacer, commlink, patch cable. Seemed like it was all there. And I was alive, so I figured my guts and brain were prolly good.

Alive. And that meant I was a 3D print. I was just *printed*. 'I think, therefore I am the most advanced figurine ever made'.

I looked back at the tube that served as both a sender and receiver of teleported human bodies. It was decidedly more elegant than what Eli threw together – but hey, it wouldn't fit in a van. The entire room looked dedicated to that machine, feeding it with cables and tubes from a dozen different hardware racks.

"Jack, seriously," Allie cut through my reverie. "You're freaking me out. Let me check you."

She held up a penlight, shining it into each of my eyes. I winced as she told me to follow it while she made circles in the air.

"How did you get here?" I asked her, staring at the beam.

"I don't see any signs of neurotrauma," she replied. "But there's obviously some memory loss. You wanted me to do this. You said you needed me to do it. That it would save you from getting killed by those mercs, and that your friends would make sure both of us were taken care of."

None of that sounded right. My friends?

Katarina.

The details came back to me like a sledgehammer to the brain. Katarina hadn't found a new asset. She just found a different way to get to Alice. I wanted to be furious at the way she – *they* – shattered whatever trust I'd manage to give them, but my head was so foggy I could hardly hold on to any one thought.

I shook my head, and two words rattled around more than any others: 'betrayal' and 'professional'. Strangely at odds with each other considering both of them made me think of Katarina.

Then the gravity of the situation finally rolled in. I was in TaoCom central, I had a job to do, and I needed to pull it together if I wanted to keep Alice safe.

"Okay, okay..." I said. "Let's just get moving. You're taking me to the terminal, right?"

Alice nodded and rushed out the door. I followed her into a dimly lit hallway. Everything from floor to ceiling had a hospital's bare, sterile look, but the dim lighting made it seem like the entire floor had been abandoned.

"This way," she said, turning a corner and stopping at a blue door that looked just like the fifteen others we'd just passed.

She pulled a palm-sized object from her pocket, swiped it over the door, and it slid open with a quiet hiss. Her TaoCom security badge, I figured.

The room beyond held exactly what I was looking for: an access point to the research department's data center. Floor-to-ceiling drive storage racks filled the back half of the room, and a central monitor displayed a login screen requesting a password, high-level ID badge, and biometric input.

None of which we had – which is where Pilky's skills came in.

"What's the security look like out there? Any patrols?" I asked Allie as I fished the commlink out of my pocket.

"I don't really know," she answered. "This isn't my sector. I work in biomedical. I don't even know what this zone is, but it looks like it's been shut down."

"I was thinking the same thing."

I used my knife to pop an access panel from the terminal and wired in the commlink. Hopefully, Pilky would know when it was active since my neurocom still wasn't working.

"Hey, can you com anyone from the crew? My neurocom isn't booting."

Alice looked at me funny.

"Not booting? Then how is your wetgear working? It must just be the NUI or something. Anyway, no, I don't have any contacts."

I guess we'd just have to wait and hope for the best. I activated the link, then paced from one side of the room to the other, my eyes never leaving the login screen on the terminal.

"Who told you that I wanted you to do this?" I asked Allie. "Because if you say it was me, then my brain did actually get scrambled."

"No, it was a woman named Katarina," Allie said. "She had GreySec credentials and told me she was helping you sort out whatever trouble you were in. She knew your whole story. Even had vids of you hanging out with her and some girl with pink hair. I figured if she was protecting you, then I could trust her."

"And she told you that I *wanted* you to get involved?"

"Yeah. And now it sounds like you didn't," she replied, the corners of her mouth drawing down. Her eyes leaned into the expression, nearly quivering as Allie quickly looked away.

"Look," I said, stopping to put my hand on Alice's arm. "I told her I didn't. And it was only because what we're doing is dangerous."

"Well, I'm here," she said, sniffing. "No changing it now."

Looking into her eyes, the barest onset of tears told me she was waiting for a very specific response. And I wanted to give that specific response.

"And I'm glad you're here," I smiled. "Now."

I wanted to ask her how she still considered me a close enough friend to take this kind of risk. I wanted to know how she could just pick up again like that. And I wanted to know if she'd missed me after I disappeared into the Quarters over a year ago.

But I didn't want to ask her here, in a badly-lit lab, with two-hundred floors worth of TaoCom corpo-rats under our feet. I coughed, looking back at the terminal.

The login screen was gone, replaced by a long list of files and directories. Breaktime was over, and I reached into my other pocket for the coil of neural interfacing patch cable that I'd brought for the data extraction.

"Nicely done, Pilky," I whispered, darting back over to the hardware.

I ran the patch cable between my isostick port and the terminal and began the transfer. With my NUI offline, I had to trust the terminal hardware to show me the transfer's status. Calculations and scans danced across the terminal display until a progress bar made an appearance. It clocked an estimated transfer time of forty-two minutes.

"Oh, hell no," I said.

"What is it, Jack?"

"We're not sitting here for another forty minutes," I replied. "I know this area looks unused, but a patrol has to come through here eventually."

I patted my sheathed knife reflexively. Sharp, sexy, and primed with a neurotoxin cartridge made to send paralyzing poison to the edge of the blade through microscopic capillaries.

It was a small comfort.

Imagining a TaoCom security squad running down the hallway with SMGs blazing made me think it wouldn't be *quite* enough if the shit hit the fan. It made me wish Eli hadn't advised against 'imaging too much tech' with his cobbled-together origin scanner – his concerns being the reason I didn't bring my new Gallardo PDW.

Allie grinned absently, almost like she'd just read my thoughts. She rushed over to a box mounted to the back wall, and stuck the device from her pocket against the lid.

The lid popped open, revealing a mini-arsenal of four automatic handguns with spare magazines. She grabbed and loaded two of the guns and then handed me one.

"TaoCom has arms lockers on high-security floors," she smiled.

"I'm sure they're wired," I said, taking the pistol and checking the chamber. "I hope that didn't set off a silent alarm."

Allie held up the little device and smiled.

"Katarina," she said. "She gave me this Lockpick to get through the lab doors without alerting security. Figured it would work there, too."

Hopefully, she was right. If not, TaoCom security would definitely be making a copious delivery of lead any minute.

I set the loaded steel on the terminal and went back to watching the progress. Twenty-nine more minutes on the progress bar, and below that, the names of files and folders zoomed by on their way from the data center to my brain:

Project MonkeyPaw...

Project Spinning Wheel...

Project Looking Glass...

Project Red Hood...

Project Golden Egg...

"What's with these names?" I asked Allie.

She looked over my shoulder and said it was just a TaoCom naming convention.

"Didn't you wonder why the secret data stream project is called 'BeanStalk'?"

"Sort of, and I still don't get it," I shrugged. "Ten minutes left on the clock."

Allie chuckled, then went back to watching the door, hot steel at the ready.

Then a second later, she gasped.

"Uh oh," she said, nodding to the door access panel which was now slowly pulsing red. "I think they're onto us."

"Dammit! They must have scoped the data transfer," I said, slamming my fist against the terminal. "Six minutes left..."

"They're probably already on this floor, Jack. I can use the Lockpick to get the door open again, but I don't know for how long."

I wasn't ready to take unnecessary risks with Allie's safety. Z would just have to be happy with whatever data I transferred so far, and if anyone questioned my judgment, it'd give me the perfect chance to remind them that I never wanted my friend here in the first place.

"Screw it," I said, yanking the patch cable and commlink from the terminal and shoving them into my jacket pockets. "We're not taking a chance."

I grabbed the loaded automatic off the terminal and bolted toward the door.

"Alright, open it. Then get back."

I took a breath. The quiet hiss of the door sliding open sounded as loud as thunder this time. If security was nearby, they must have heard it.

I leaned out to peek, then snapped back into the room. Nothing out there yet.

"Let's go," I whispered, leading the way down the hall.

The corridor had been dimly lit before they cut the lights. Then they cut the lights. My non-functioning NUI couldn't adjust and everything in front of me turned to shadows and rough shapes.

We reached the intersection, and I was now blind in four directions. Instinctively, I tried to power on the flashlight on my wetgear finger, but the new model didn't have one.

Interesting how you can really miss the small things.

"Can you see?" I asked Allie. "Too dark for me."

She nodded – as far as I could tell – and leaned out into the intersection.

"It's clear," she whispered back. "Let me go ahead."

Allie took off down the corridor before I could protest, and I followed the vague outline of her body deeper into the darkness.

"Stop!" a deep voice shattered the silence from the far end of the hall.

I raised my weapon, but there was nothing to see. Until Allie fired a shot.

The muzzle flash burned my eyes with a motionless image of the scene: Allie ducking and firing straight ahead at a trio of TaoCom security guards in dark corpo suits and tactical visors. Each one of them had a submachine gun trained in our direction.

I didn't need a NUI notification to recognize the adrenaline spike. Using the lingering retina burn as a reference, I raised my own pistol and squeezed off three shots.

It was like watching some kind of slow-moving slide show. Each flash from my muzzle painted a new picture in my eyes. Allie diving to the side of the corridor; two of the guards reeling backward; their weapons suspended in the air on their way to the floor.

Then the third guard fired back, bathing the entire scene in blinding white.

I dove to the ground, weapon forward, and continued pulling the trigger. By the time I'd emptied the magazine, no one was firing back.

"Allie! Dammit. I can't see anything," I growled.

"They're all down," she said, grabbing my free arm and pulling me to my feet. "Come on."

She pulled me past the shadows of three bodies on the ground...then one of their arms moved. I was too slow to react – he fired a single shot, and Allie let go of my arm.

Another image painted my vision in burning white light. One of the guards held his sidearm leveled at Alice. I threw my empty pistol at his face and heard it connect. My hand went for my knife and lunged at the man's fading image. Landing on him, I drove the MMK's blade into his stomach.

The neurotoxin did the rest. I heard his weapon drop to the floor and felt every part of him tighten, shake, and then go limp beneath me.

"Allie?" I yelled.

"This way," she said. "Hurry."

When she grabbed my arm this time, her hand felt wet. Another twenty steps down the corridor, and we finally stopped. I heard a door slide open and Allie pulled me inside.

She closed the door and worked her fingers over a control terminal on the wall. A moment later, the overhead lights kicked on. I saw the transporter, its various lights and readouts coming back to life. Allie stood next to an open access panel, the wall around it covered in bloody handprints.

She turned and smiled as if to apologize for something. Dark blood covered her from her abdomen to her knees.

"Oh shit!" I gasped and ran to her.

I pressed my hand against the bullet wound in her stomach, and she nearly screamed.

"Pressure," I stammered. "Put pressure…"

"No," she moaned. "The blood…"

It was almost black. The bullet must have gone through her liver. I tried to help Allie stay on her feet, but she was getting heavier. I lowered her to the floor.

"Keep your damn eyes open, Allie! I'm trying to think of something here!"

I ran frantically around the room, looking for a medkit. Nothing. The corpo bastards put arms lockers, but didn't bother providing first aid supplies.

Glancing back to Allie, she was completely motionless on the floor.

"No, no, no…" I said, more of a command than a plea.

I grabbed her wrists, and dragged her over to the transporter. With ample help from my cybernetic limbs, I hefted her into the tube and slammed the lid.

She was dying, but data doesn't experience the passage of time, right? That was my thinking as I punched through the command console on the transporter. A few seconds later, I'd set the last point of origin as the new destination and initiated the transport.

By now, Z should have rerouted that address from Eli's origin scanner in the van to the brainer that was intended to hold my data in limbo.

Behind me, the door panel chimed, then buzzed. Allie must have locked the door somehow – a small comfort considering that could only buy me a few more minutes.

Ah, I really fragged this up. Loud pounding against the door served as perfect punctuation to the thought.

I watched the imagers and engram scanners working through a monitor on the command console. Progress bars filled, and status updates scrolled over an image of Alice, completely still and ghostly white. I stood, sweating, shaking, just hoping it would finish before they made it through the door.

The console chimed, the notifications stopped, and one final message flashed across the screen:

BALANCING

The tube roared for an instant, the sound of some very visceral technology kicking in. Then Alice was no longer on the monitor. I ripped open the tube's lid, unleashing the smell of ionized air and medical sanitizer, and she was gone.

"I'm sorry, Allie," I whispered. "I really hope that worked."

I heaved a deep breath, knowing well enough that there were still other problems to contend with. Z was only expecting to intercept one human's worth of transporter data. Who the hell knew what would happen if I tried to transport now.

Z might not receive the transmission at all. Or it could kill the brainer, and *everything* would be lost – Allie, me, and the damn intel in my brain partition.

Desperate measures. I slapped the commlink onto the transporter terminal and wired it in, piggybacking my pocket 'facer on the same port.

If my luck was still holding out, Pilky would tap into the new connection, and I could inject some breadcrumbs.

I tapped out a message on my 'facer and pushed it through the link.

NCOM DOWN. SENT AL INSTEAD. I AM STUCK. NEED NEW DESTINATION?!?! -J

Then I waited. More pounding on the door rang out. Pretty soon, they'd just bypass the lock. Or blow the damn door open with breaching charges.

Nothing came back on my 'facer or the terminal. I wracked my brain for any other plan of escape.

Then Pilky came through, yet again. The console monitor shifted from screen to screen, apparently under his control. Settings changed, maps and coordinates flew by, then everything stopped. The monitor showed a ping on the map somewhere on the west side of Hope along with a single button to initialize a transport.

"Guess anywhere is better than here."

I pocketed my 'facer, hit the button on the console, and climbed into the tube. Lights and scanners came to life as soon as I slammed the lid shut over me.

Everything went black again.

Chapter Twenty-Seven

FORMLESS

T his time was different.

I was aware. Aware of being…disassociated was the word Z used. I had none of my familiar senses, but I still felt the presence of thoughts and ideas. I could tell I was moving, but couldn't feel the typical signs of movement. No rushing wind. No tensing muscles.

I just knew. It's like how a dreamer can see someone who totally doesn't look like a person, but they *know* it's supposed to be that person. Everything around me was like that. All things were form-less but completely clear in meaning.

Is this what it feels like when some experimental engram scanner scrambles your brain?

A vastness of ideas slid past me, and I just observed, like an unmoving stone in a river experiencing a thousand miles of land through the water's touch. I couldn't hold on to any of it – nor did I want to.

Until a thought of Alice coalesced. I could sense her form, pale and lifeless, covered in blood. I reached out to grab her, but I had nothing to catch her with. I tried to move closer, but there was no distance to cover.

And suddenly, I was part of that sensation. I was the formless Alice, or part of it. And I imagined her bloody form regaining color, becoming whole again. The form changed and became the Allie I remembered from my dreams. The one who would visit me after school and cheer me up.

She smiled, she laughed. She was alive. We held hands and talked about her dreams of science and getting away from the mega. How she would work in an orbital lab or somewhere even farther from this place. And how she wanted me to go with her.

Then I felt her drifting away. There was no force to resist, no aggressor to fight. She was just caught in the current of formless thoughts.

The void she left filled up again with other blurred faces. Was that Z and Eli? They were standing over a brainer strapped into a NetOps chair. Oh, that's right...the operation. They must be waiting for the transfer.

I slid inside the brainer's mind, or it felt like that's what I was doing. I didn't see Alice inside that place, but that's where she was supposed to be. Her and the stolen data from the lab, captured and stored. Safe.

I didn't want the data. I wanted Alice back. So, I gave the place what it was waiting for, hoping that I could leave and search for her.

I slid back out of that mind and into the formless. How could I search without senses? I couldn't look for Allie. I couldn't even call out her name so she could find me.

Again, there was darkness.

Chapter Twenty-Eight

THE DESTINATION

"Dammit, Vikk! Hold them off! We just finished reviving her!"

Katarina's voice cut through the void. My NUI kicked on, and darkness lit up with startup screens and notifications.

"Two more TaoCom units just showed up out front," a man's voice called out from farther away.

I could hear gunshots. A lot of gunshots. My NUI finished initializing, but I wasn't so sure I cared. I wanted to keep lying down. And I was hungry.

"Shit, doc!" Katarina yelled. "We are out of time! Get her out of that tube...NOW!"

Then someone slapped me in the face.

"Jack, *chica*, you need to wake up. *Necesitamos movernos.*"

I opened my eyes. A blurry man with a mouthful of gold teeth stared back. "She is awake, Miss..eh...Captain Guterres!"

The ripping sound of submachine gun fire echoed around me in bursts.

"Get her on her feet, Ricardo!"

Another burst of gunfire, and I felt a shower of hot brass casings hit my chest and arms.

"Ah, *Dios mio*," Ricardo mumbled, brushing the casings off me.

"What the hell is going on?" I managed to ask.

Ricardo grabbed my shoulders and sat me up. More blurry figures moved around the tube, all of them armed.

"Believe me," Ricardo yelled over another staccato burst, "I do not know. But we need to go and...I first need you to stand up."

He helped me out of the tube-shaped transporter station. But it had to be a different transporter. I was in a large open bay, like some sort of storage facility, not the sterile room of the TaoCom lab.

Katarina ran to me and grabbed my shoulders, her smoking submachine gun dangling from a three-point sling. "Jack, I need you lucid and operational," she said, looking directly into my eyes. "Do you remember me?"

Long brown hair, cinnamon skin, features like a bird of prey. I completely remember that look. Only difference was she was wearing some kind of black headset-slash-visor that covered her eyes and ears.

"Katarina," I said, stretching my neck.

I flinched and hunched down as a volley of bullets tore through the nearby wall, and spears of light streamed in from the ragged holes.

"Right. Good enough."

She reached into a green duffle bag on the ground and pulled out a blue-and-black Gallardo PDW. I recognized it. Katarina shoved it into my hands before shouldering her own weapon.

"It's loaded, but I don't want you shooting any of us in the back," she said. "You don't shoot unless someone in a TaoCom uniform is right on top of you, clear?"

"Yeah, clear."

Maybe not clear, but getting there. I was remembering more, and even though I had no idea where I was, I had a pretty good clue about how I got there. I remember Ricardo from the docshop, and she'd mentioned Vikk. I also noticed that Katarina was wearing a brown and gray camouflage jumpsuit – the first time I'd seen her not wearing a GreySec uniform.

Katarina slapped me on the shoulder and motioned for me to follow.

I gathered more details between flinching and crouching my way through incoming waves of bullets. We were definitely in a storage building, something big enough to park a few cargo trucks in. There were stacks of crates everywhere, many of them pocked with bullet holes that I assumed were very recent. I also saw a lot of bodies in TaoCom uniforms on the floor.

We made our way toward an open roll-up door in the far wall; one of six, but it was the only door open to the hazy daylight outside.

It wasn't just Katarina and doc beside me. There were two more with us, but they had on masks so I couldn't make them out. One had orange hair, the other's head was shaved clean and covered in ink. Both wore the same visor setup over their eyes and ears as Katarina.

"Vikk," Katarina said, "Time to clear a path. We have the asset."

Oh, am I an asset now? I ducked behind the edge of the open door and peeked out. The skyline told me it was the middle of the day, but the overcity's shadow made it seem more like dusk around the building. Sheets of light rain danced on a quartet of black TaoCom trucks parked at angles twenty meters out in the parking lot.

At least a dozen of their corpo goombas were out there, too, a mix of 'executive protection' types in suits and heavies decked out in red TaoCom security armor. They alternated between firing into the doorway and inching closer to us, using whatever they could find for cover.

We would have been skitz-out-of-luck if a seven-foot-tall cyber-golem hadn't run from behind the building, unleashing his unique version of hell. But he did, and it was a glorious sight to wake up to.

Vikk came into the scene hard, shouldering one of the TaoCom trucks at a full sprint, rolling it sideways halfway across the parking lot. The vehicle took out three of the shooters who were too slow to avoid a brutal crushing.

The golem followed up with a volley of flechettes from his right knuckles, the precision fire dropping another three TaoCom flunkies to the dirt.

"Now!" Katarina yelled, opening fire with her SMG and pushing out into the parking lot.

Vikk made the exit almost trivial by drawing all the hostile fire. Katarina and the others were able to pick off the attackers one by one as we moved. The two that gave up and tried to beat feet out of the parking lot, she shot in the back.

Doc Ricardo ushered me toward an armored four-door pickup truck, heavily modified with roll bars up top and gate crashers in the front. He opened the rear door for me while Katarina and crew circled around the truck, weapons at the ready.

"Get in, Vikk!" she yelled, pushing me into the back seat.

The golem hoisted himself into the bed of the truck and grabbed the roll cage like a set of handlebars.

"Contact front!" the bald guy yelled before cutting loose with his rifle.

Through the windshield, I watched three more TaoCom trucks round a corner and speed toward us, rooster tails of rainwater kicking up behind them. My grip tightened on the PDW, and I moved to jump back out of the vehicle.

Katarina put her arm out to block me and said: "Tandy's got this."

A black ARV ripped through the sky overhead and hovered just ahead of our truck. The air filled with a shrill electric whine as bright red tracer rounds poured out of its bow and into the oncoming vehicles.

All three trucks swerved, popped full of smoking holes. Their metal bodies shredded and ripped free of their frames. Then the trucks outright exploded.

"Frag yeah!" the orange-haired dude yelled from the other side of our truck.

I couldn't fault his enthusiasm.

"Nice job, Tan," Katarina said, waving me over in the bench seat so she could climb in. "Asset secure, we're oscar. Nap CAS...egress beta-four."

Baldy climbed into the driver's seat, and Doc Ricardo took shotgun. Katarina finished talking to herself before climbing in next to me. The truck fired up, and we were moving with Vikk in the back, riding the truck like a scooter, and orange hair crouched behind him.

"Who are you talking to?" I asked Katarina.

She pulled off the headset thing and handed it to me. It reminded me of the augmented visors the Luckies sometimes used during their jobs.

"Built-in tactical comms," she explained. "Completely off MiFi. Don't want to use neurocoms when you're robbing the people who own the network."

"Hm. Good point," I said, holding the visor up to my eyes.

Everything had a yellow tint through the lenses, but the view was crystal sharp. I swiveled my head and noticed that every occupant of the car had a white outline – some kind of built-in target designator. More features than the Luckies' gear I'd used before.

I handed the device back to Katarina, then some stray thought tickled at the back of my mind. Then the tickle exploded to fill my brain.

"Hey!" I said, shocked by the memory that suddenly surfaced. "Where's Alice?"

"What?" Katarina asked, cocking her head back. "Look, I know you're probably pissed about her getting involved, but we can discuss the morals and ethics of that later."

"No...I sent her through the transporter. I fragging...you know...transmitted her!"

Katarina paused, staring at me for a long moment.

"I'm sorry, Jack. I really have no clue what you're talking about. If this is about the transporters, that's all Z and Pilky. I don't do that kind of tech."

I could feel my heart sinking, trading places with the guts rising up to my throat.

"They didn't say anything about storing her data? Reprinting her? Nothing?"

Katarina shook her head. "Jack, we'll get that sorted out. But if I were you, I'd be more worried about what you missed in the last three weeks."

"Huh? What?" My organs continued shuffling.

"You've been sitting in that machine for three weeks. I mean, your 'data' was. Cached, buffered, whatever. It took a lot of planning to get in there. And some time."

"Three weeks," I whispered.

"Yup," Katarina grinned. "Weirdest fraggin' rescue mission I've ever been on. I had to *print* you." She hesitated, then added: "And that was after I helped turn your body over to HighCastle for the bounty."

I shot her a very disapproving look.

"Your original body," she said, holding up her hand as if to stop me from protesting. "You weren't using it. And it wasn't for the scrip. We did it so that TaoCom would stop looking for you." She grinned. "The payout was just a bonus."

"At least I don't owe you anything for the upgrades now," I said, turning my head toward the rain-flecked window.

I spotted the ARV's shadow following us along the wet road. Beyond it, the streets and storefronts of the mega flowed by. Hope looked different somehow.

"Wait, we're in Downtown South," I said, noticing the landmarks as we passed. "The streets are practically empty. Where is everyone?"

"After the Skypillar operation, the GCs panicked. Afraid their secrets had gotten out. They locked down most of the city for the last two weeks. And they boosted security around any facility that had to do with the transporters. That's why we had to wait to extract you."

"Looks like it's still in lockdown to me."

"People are still afraid to go out," Katarina said. "The first few days were..."

"A fraggin' massacre," Baldy said from the front seat.

"Locking down millions of people is not easy," Katarina nodded. "It turned into street warfare overnight. GreySec scored more than a few new contracts because of it. I'm not the only one who resigned because of what came after."

"You left the corporation?" I asked. "What about your connections and supply hookups?"

Katarina shrugged. "We can still get our hands on hardware. Like that refurbished ARV we liberated from the HMPD substation," she shot me a wry grin. "Tandy even flies it."

"I was wondering about that. How did…"

"Drugs," she said. "Doc found a mix of nootropics that keeps her condition in check. Mostly."

Well damn, everyone's been busy while I was just chilling in a memory bank.

"Almost to the tunnel, Captain," Mohawk called out from the front seat.

"Captain?" I asked. "Still holding on to that rank and title, then?"

"I did earn it," Katarina raised her eyebrow. "I did two tours in Brazil, and commanded a GreySec company in the Fulda Gap before I turned HMPD. Besides, people remember it. Getting goons and mercs to call me 'Miss Guterres' was harder than you might think."

"They're not the types who stand on ceremony," I chuckled. "'Captain' is more fitting anyway."

The truck suddenly cut to the right, off the main road, and down a barren ramp that was never meant for vehicles. The ramp led us through a huge culvert under the street that opened into a wide part of the drainage canal system.

Baldy steered us through the canal for about a hundred yards, then into a pitch-black tunnel of com-crete running under street level. Once inside, the truck's cabin filled with an almost deafening roar.

"What the hell is that?" I yelled over the noise.

Katarina pointed backward, and I turned to look out the rear window. Beyond Vikk and the truck's tailgate, the black ARV hugged the road right on our ass.

"Thrust motors," Katarina yelled. "They echo like hell in this tunnel."

The black windscreen of the flying vehicle turned translucent, and Tandy waved from the pilot's chair. I waved back at the smiling girl with vivid pink hair before facing forward in my seat.

"Hell, she's good. This tunnel is barely big enough for that thing," I said.

"She's *really* good," Katarina agreed. "Turns out she was training in simulations without telling anyone."

Amazing. Tandy had to be thrilled to be off phantom duty. Running around the city spoofing surveillance systems bored the hell out of her, and flying a gunship had to be infinitely more exciting.

The tunnel terminated in a huge metal door which was already sliding down into the floor by the time our headlights brought it into view. The truck – and the ARV behind it – barely slowed down as we passed through.

Shortly beyond the door, we came to a stop in a massive open chamber. It was every bit a large underground parking lot. It even had a few dormant trucks, sedans, and bikes lined up along the back wall.

Baldy parked us in line with the other rides, while I watched Tandy make a perfect landing through the side window.

"This is the sub-basement of one of the empty buildings in the redevelopment zone," Katarina explained. "We sealed this off and removed it from the engineering records, just like with the Undercroft."

"I'm guessing that's where we're going," I said.

"Yeah, this is our new private entrance and motorpool."

Everyone piled out of the truck, and Tandy bounced over from the parked ARV. She looked a bit strange in a gray flight suit, considering her black and neon pink hair in an elaborate, spiky do.

"Jack!" she squealed, grabbing me for a hug. "I knew you'd make it!"

"Pfft. Not without your help, Tan. You're really good with that thing."

"Oh...my...globs. It is *so* much fun," she flashed a surprisingly wicked grin. "You saw me shred those corpo skitzheads, right?"

I laughed, and she unzipped her flight suit all the way down to reveal a bright pink dress over a black bodcon suit covered in little skulls. She stepped out of the crumpled flight suit and pulled the hem of the dress down.

"Oh, that's the Tandy I remember," I said.

"Huh?" she grunted, throwing the suit in the truck's backseat like an afterthought.

I just chuckled and shook my head, then Katarina waved me over toward a door set into the wall.

"Let's get inside," she said. "Z's dying to see you."

Chapter Twenty-Nine

THE DEBRIEF

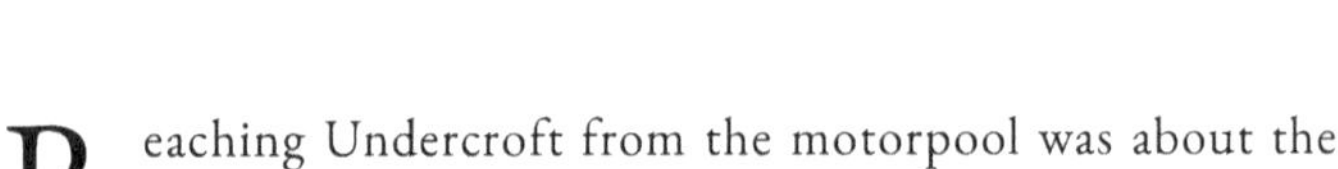

Reaching Undercroft from the motorpool was about the same as entering from the drainage canals. Dark tunnels, remote actuated doors, and armed guards.

The brilliance of the huge hideout wasn't lost on me. A few choke point entrances, heavily defended, and probably fifty feet of dirt and solid foundations overhead. If someone wanted to get in, they'd have to drop a tunneling missile on the place, and even corpos wouldn't do that kind of damage to their own city.

Plus, they'd have to find the place first.

Once inside, Tandy and the others broke off to do their own things while Katarina led me through the cylindrical arrangement of familiar shop fronts. The most noticeable difference from my last visit was the increase in foot traffic.

It was like everyone who was afraid to wander the streets had decided to pack themselves into the underground. Along with the mercs and 'lancers, there seemed to be quite a few street-level civilians just looking for a place to socialize and grab a shot of vodka or a can of HeadRush. A new cantina, little more than an improvised bar counter surrounded by an eclectic mix of tables, had even popped up in the center of the bottom floor to accommodate all the extra patrons.

We bypassed the crowds to reach the unassuming entrance to the Undercroft's private NetOps suite.

It was the kind of environment I was already used to seeing Zoroaster in. Walls of networking hardware, thick trunks of cabling, and glowing terminals and monitors filled a chamber that was at least twice as big as the one in the fallout shelter. It also had three NetOps chairs in the center, one of which was occupied by Pilky. The Brit was dead still, probably tranced out for a long DarkNet dive.

Z himself was standing nearby, staring into a handheld slate. When he turned to greet us, I was surprised to see him wearing bright – and rather trendy – street clothes underneath his brown duster instead of the usual NetOps suit.

Katarina excused herself and disappeared back into the Undercroft's array of stalls and storefronts.

"Jack," Z smiled, drawing out the name. "It's about time."

I wasn't sure how to process that smile. A hard reset on trust makes it tough to read a person that you thought was watching out for you. But I was determined that if Z wanted me around, he was going to help get Alice back. I just had to set up the pieces.

"You're telling me," I said, stepping toe-to-toe with the tall psycher and his perfect teeth. "Now, do me a favor and get your intel out of my brain so we can square up this arrangement."

Z raised an eyebrow. "We already have the intel, Jack."

"What? *How?*" I snapped. Was my leverage already falling out from under me?

Z held up his hands and waited for me to take a breath before continuing.

"I know it wasn't a perfect operation," he said. "But I can answer your questions. One at a time, if you'll let me."

I stared into his eyes, trying to remember why – and if – I trusted him. He didn't look confused any more. If anything, he looked concerned.

I nodded to let him know I was ready to listen.

"First of all, Eli came through as promised. Your father is in Lonestar," Z said. "He was released from his servitude contract last week, and Eli's people are taking care of him. We decided it was best not to bring him to Hope until tensions in the city ease a little."

I'd been hoping for a reunion – some real, positive outcome to grab hold of – but maybe it was better that Dad was somewhere safe. I wasn't ready to celebrate anyway. Too many people were still in trouble – or worse – and I couldn't let go of that fact.

"And the data I jacked from TaoCom?"

"After you asked for a new destination and transmitted yourself, the data transferred into the brainer that we'd set up to store you. Thousands of files straight from the TaoCom research department's secure storage."

"No, Z…I sent *Alice* back to you, not the data. I put her in the transporter and sent her to the network address you gave me."

Z cocked his head, confused again. "Well, if that's the case, then I don't have as many answers as I thought I did."

"Stellar," I sighed.

"What I do know is that my theory was right. You do have a unique connection to the BeanStalk. And I believe, now more than ever, that if we had tried to send anyone other than you through Eli's transporter, they wouldn't have made it."

Did that mean Alice couldn't have made it? She wasn't going to survive that gunshot, so what I did was better than doing nothing at all, right?

Z stopped pacing and leaned against Pilky's NetOps chair.

"We didn't know why you requested a new destination, but we trusted you had a good reason. Pilky had to find something on zero notice that would work. There was a Project LookingGlass manifest in the new data showing a transporter unit in a facility at street level."

"So what, 'LookingGlass' is the transporter deal?" I asked. "'BeanStalk', now 'LookingGlass'. Frag me with these names. And that transporter was in the warehouse where Katarina picked me up, right?"

"Yes. It was our best option, but sending you to a questionable transporter unit inside a highly-guarded TaoCom facility was not ideal. So, Pilky came up with a workaround and stored you in the transporter's cache. Then he wiped the transporter log data so TaoCom couldn't tell who was transported or where."

"Better than printing out randomly in a warehouse full of TaoCom flunkies, I guess."

"You would not have been well received." Z grinned. "But this way, we could plan and mount a recovery op. Being able to extract you at the most opportune time is an altogether rare advantage in these situations, and we were glad to have it."

"I'm surprised Katarina was willing to come get me if you already had the data."

Z sighed in mock exasperation before walking over to a shelf on the wall and pulling down two cans of HeadRush. He threw one at me, and cracked open the other.

"There was some tension before you left," he said, following with a long swig from the can. "Katarina was rightfully angry about losing

Mallus. That incident convinced her that you weren't going to make it in our crew."

I opened the HeadRush and took a slow sip. I certainly hadn't forgiven myself for getting Mallus killed. In a twisted way, I was thankful for all of the more pressing issues that helped keep that from the front of my mind.

Z continued: "I was just as angry at Katarina when I realized she recruited your friend as our asset inside the corporation. That put us at odds for a few days as well, but in time she realized it may not have been the best decision. After that, Katarina was the most adamant about recovering you as quickly as possible. She insisted that she lead the rescue team."

"Guess a lot can happen to a person in three weeks," I said, staring into the mouth of the HeadRush can.

"Those are the facts at hand, Jack. What's still unanswered is how you managed to get the stolen data into the brainer while you arrived in a completely different location. If we can answer that question, I think it will lead us to your friend."

"I put Allie in the tube and transmitted her. Then I got inside the tube and transmitted myself to the destination Pilky found. I didn't *do* anything, Z."

"Nothing that you were aware of at the time," Z added. "Let me show you something."

He walked to another set of shelves nestled between tall network hardware racks. After pushing various boxes and components aside, he returned with a small box in his hands.

He opened the box. Inside was a small disc, roughly the size of an old-world metal coin, with a hexagon-shaped processor core in the middle.

"This is your puck implant, Jack."

I instinctively grabbed the back of my neck, and Z grinned.

"I took the liberty of removing it from your body before we handed it over to HighCastle for the bounty. Less for them to discover from an autopsy, and an opportunity for us to examine the implant *ex vivo*."

"You know, I just can't get enough of hearing about my corpse." I sighed. "But go on. Did you find anything out?"

"Oh, yes," Z smiled. "And with help from the data you extracted from TaoCom, we've turned a lot of speculation into a working theory. That includes confirming that it is powered by a quantum processor, as Eli first suggested.

"TaoCom's quantum computing tech has come a long way since this was built, but your puck is still quite incredible. It's infinitely more complex than a standard neurocom interface, able to augment your nervous system, and correct for neurological birth defects."

Z handed me the box, and I plucked out the tiny wafer. This is what's been keeping me alive all these years. It's what Mom and Dad practically sold their souls to obtain.

"Now, here's the larger discovery that came from the TaoCom files," Z said, pacing. "The BeanStalk is actually a form of quantum entanglement telecommunication. It's not a signal or a transmission in the traditional sense."

"Like everyone was saying – carrierless and secure," I said, still examining the puck between my fingers.

"Any node that's part of this BeanStalk network is inexorably linked to other nodes – perhaps *all* other nodes – at the sub-atomic level. That's why I could never crack the BeanStalk itself, only the conventional technology connected to its quantum nodes."

"It sounds like the BeanStalk isn't even real. It's just...a metaphor," I said.

"Exactly right," Z said. "And that's why you're able to 'see' a sort of augmented reality rendering of the BeanStalk. As we assumed earlier, it's not *real* in any physical sense. It's simply a representation of the various interconnected quantum nodes most likely used for troubleshooting the system."

"And if I'm seeing what TaoCom sees...and I have a TaoCom-built quantum computer hooked to my brain..."

"The logical assumption is that your puck connects you to the BeanStalk network. It would explain how data from the stream first found its way into your brain partition. And quite possibly how the exfiltrated TaoCom data ended up reaching us, even when you didn't."

"So I'm a 'node', then." I sighed. "I sent the data straight from my partition into your brainer."

I put the puck back into its little box, shut the lid, and tossed the whole mess onto one of the empty chairs. As interesting as it was, getting that can of HeadRush back into my hands felt like a higher priority. I grabbed the drink off the rolling table and took a long swig.

"That would be my guess," Z said. "But it would imply that you can exert influence over the data in the quantum stream, either consciously or subconsciously. That presents an entirely different puzzle to be solved.

"First, we should determine the extent of this connection between your implant and the BeanStalk. Your quantum tech is obviously very small. And two decades old. I'm not even certain if the connection was an intentional part of the design or just some accidental byproduct of TaoCom's quantum technology."

"Does it really matter?" I asked.

"Perhaps. I'm sure you'd agree that a carrierless, traceless connection to the Hope Consortium's most secure and secretive data stream would be useful."

I wondered if Z was actually a nice guy or if he was so cordial because I always managed to be 'useful'.

About then, the HeadRush really started kicking in. I rubbed my temples, remembering the huge list of other concerns looming over me. Allie, my father, Mallus – it was all closing in, and I felt my mouth go dry and my skin go cold.

Then the numbness came. I don't know if I'd learned how to do it or if it was just something that happened, but the numbness started when I was working with the Luckies. When things got too intense, it kept me sane by putting a wall between my thoughts and all the pressure and fear outside.

I welcomed the numbness. I couldn't afford to cry or curl up on the floor back then, any more than I could afford to now. What I needed to do was pay attention, come up with a plan, and keep it together.

A different kind of pain shot through my gut and reminded me of something else I needed to do.

"Hey, Z?" I asked. "Got any food in here? I haven't eaten in three weeks."

Chapter Thirty

SIMILARITIES

Once Zoroaster confessed that he hadn't been out of the NetOps suite in at least ten hours, he suggested we hit up one of the Undercroft's vendors for a bite. His vote was for the teppanyaki stand on the bottom floor, but I wanted to check out our options.

Our topics were less severe as we walked around the stands. I told Z about my neurocom malfunction, and he said he would check the error logs when we got back. I asked him what Pilky was doing that required a medically-induced sleep state – tranced, the psychers call it – and Z said he was resting his body during a 72-hour dive in the DarkNet.

And I finally worked myself up to ask what he knew about Mallus. Even though I assumed by this point he had to be dead, Z said they were holding out hope until a body turned up.

We ultimately doubled back to the teppanyaki stand that Z first suggested. Admittedly, the slices of meat cooking on the flattop smelled pretty damn good, and I loved a bowl of sticky rice even when I'm not starving.

The stand was right next to the pop-up cantina in the middle of the bottom floor, so I ordered a couple of beers while Z grabbed the chow.

Even with the mulling crowd, we were able to find an empty table to sit at and enjoy our meal – although I suspected Z's position as a cofounder of the Undercroft made getting a seat a foregone conclusion.

The meat was juicy and had a strong taste of sugar and soy sauce. It lacked that gamey quality of real flesh that I'd tasted the few other times I'd had real meat.

"This can't be feral," I said, washing it down with a swig of beer.

"No, it's authentic New Texas beef," Z grinned. "And you'll want to thank Eli for that, too."

"Like cow?" I said. "First time for me."

"There's a reason I suggested it," Z laughed. "I always make sure this stand gets a supply of real meat. It's expensive, but some of our guests appreciate it."

I didn't say another word until my bowl of rice and meat was completely clean. An empty stomach probably made the food taste even better, and it was pretty delicious in the first place.

I took the final pull from the plastic cup of beer and leaned back in my chair.

"I've been thinking about the data," I said. "And you saying that I might have...I dunno...told it to go into the brainer."

"Yes," Z said, waving two fingers at the bartender to signal another round.

"I had a dream right before Ricardo and Katarina dragged me out of that tube. Except now you've got me thinking that maybe it wasn't a dream. I couldn't see anything, but it's like I could feel all these forms and ideas."

"That sounds a lot like psyching," Z said. "Especially when you're tranced. It's full consciousness in a completely alien sensory state. Takes a lot of getting used to."

"Yeah, right on. In the dream – or whatever it was – I actually felt myself enter the brainer's mind. And I wanted to give it the data so I could go find Allie."

Z smiled and clapped his hands.

"Well, I'm glad you remember that, Jack. Because it sounds like you were psyching on the BeanStalk and didn't even know it. Maybe you know more about this connection than you think – you just need the right context."

"That's what worries me, Z. It wasn't the only thing that happened while I was there. I also saw Alice. Or I felt her, whatever the term is. At first she was exactly like when I put her in the transporter. Then I wanted her to be healed and it felt like she was."

Z cocked his head. He leaned in and didn't even notice when the barkeep put two more cups of beer in front of us.

"But then I thought about when we were kids," I continued. "And how she wanted to work in space someday. In an orbital lab or maybe a colony. And when I thought about that, she just...faded away."

Z stared at me for a long moment, processing. He leaned back, then coughed. "Well..." he trailed off.

"You think I sent her into space, don't you?"

"I don't know," he said. "But we're really at a point now where 'anything is possible' isn't just a platitude."

"You said there was a list...a manifest of transporters, right? Does TaoCom have any LookingGlass transporters in orbit?"

Z licked his lips and blinked. Could he not tell how freakin' anxious I was to get through these questions?

"According to the manifest," he said, tenting his fingers on the table in front of him, "Project LookingGlass has two off-world prototype units online. One is aboard the orbital station SkyHaven. The other is on Mars."

That's no good. The corpo-led Mars project didn't get a ton of publicity, but as far as I knew, the colony was basically a campsite in an endless, horrifying, desert. And SkyHaven? A HighCastle facility in orbit. High-level execs only. That wouldn't be any better.

"Nah," I said, waving it off. "I couldn't have sent her there. Not without knowing what I was doing. That's nutso. Maybe she's just...buffered in one of the other LookingGlass machines. Like I was."

Z shrugged and nodded, "Well, that's certainly worth looking into. As soon as Pilky comes out of his dive, I'll see if he can check into that."

My leg bounced anxiously as I grabbed up a fresh beer and drank it down.

"Jack, I know you probably want to rest," Z said, his eyes flicking over to my shaking leg, "but if you're ready to start exploring this..."

"Let's go. Let's do it," I cut in. "I'm not tired. If anything, I'm wired. And I need to find out what happened to Alice."

Zoroaster grinned, downed his second beer, and stood.

"After you," he said, gesturing back toward the NetOps suite.

Chapter Thirty-One

THE CALL

We discussed plans to move my father to Hope during the walk back to the NetOps suite. I agreed with Z that keeping him out of the mega was the safest option, even though the corporations considered me dead.

The crew had thought ahead far enough that arrangements had already been made to house him either at the garage fallout shelter or in one of their private rooms in the Undercroft itself. The final decision would depend on the prevailing situation when he arrived.

"Thank you for taking care of all that," I told Z while climbing into the NetOps chair next to the still-tranced Pilky. "It's actually more than you promised, and I'm not used to that."

"You're welcome, Jack. Hopefully, it will remind you that we're working together here. You are part of this crew, despite some early mistakes."

"Is there any way I can talk to him?" I asked.

"Of course, Jack. On a secure hardline, of course. Your neurocom is still masked, but we don't want to take chances."

I nodded, and I couldn't help but crack a smile. I hadn't talked to my dad in about four months. That was the last time he'd been up for 'visitation', which really meant pulling him off of work rotation long enough to make a point-to-point vid call.

"I'll com Eli's assistant right now and have him put your father in front of a terminal," Z said.

His eyes flashed green, and he stared blankly toward the wall for a moment before returning his attention to me. "There we go," he smiled. "He's bringing him to a secure terminal. Let's just run a few quick scans on your wetgear while we wait."

Maybe Z looked so genuine all the time because he really was. A strange thought, but the evidence was mounting. I agreed to the scans and hopped into a vacant NetOps chair.

"Alright, you know the drill. Couple of cables, then I'll run diagnostics."

Z wired me into the NetOps hardware, as he'd done many times after we first met. He initiated his scans and silently pored over data displaying on his handheld slate.

I felt relaxed in the NetOps chair – far more than I had been the first few times Z analyzed me. But now, fed and caught up with the last three weeks of missing time, I actually started to drift off. A series of notification chimes broke me from my reverie.

"You're done," Z said. "I'll look through these while you speak to your father."

The psycher rolled a metal stool in front of a large screen set into the racks of NetOps hardware and beckoned me over.

I sank into the spongy padded seat while Z entered commands into the terminal. A second later, the screen displayed 'connecting...' and my stomach instantly felt glitchy.

"It's all yours," Z said before walking back to the other side of the room to attend to the still-tranced Pilky.

I took a breath, swallowed, and the screen flicked over to a worn face that I could hardly recognize.

His blue eyes seemed like they'd grown dimmer. Sunken into dark caverns in a face that looked wrinkled beyond its years. A few years of aging looked more like a few decades.

"Jack?" my father asked.

"Yeah, dad." Tears formed in my eyes the second the words left my tongue. I laughed, but it came out as more of a sob. I waited for him to say something else.

A long pause, and then: "They won't tell me how this happened, Jack."

I coughed through the continuing tears, then wiped my sleeve across my face. "What do you mean?"

"My contract," he said. "They said you worked out a release. But...how, Jack? What did you do?"

The glitches in my stomach turned to rocks. What was going on here?

"What did I *do*? I...I got you out of servitude, dad. I'm going to get you home."

Dad shook his head, an almost imperceptible gesture, but easy enough to read. Harder to understand, though. My father had always been supportive. Even optimistic, considering the circumstances of the past. This didn't seem like him.

He stared at me through the monitor for another long moment. "Nothing is free, Jack. *Nothing.*"

The rocks in my stomach exploded.

"*You're* free, dad!" I shouted. "*You're free!* What in the hell is wrong with you? What did they do to you?"

He opened his mouth to answer, and the screen flicked again. My father disappeared.

The image changed to a darker room in a much darker place. The unfamiliar, worn face was replaced with one I wouldn't forget.

Goodwin. The Overwatch bastard.

"Hello, Jacqueline," he smiled.

It wasn't the same smile he'd used to manipulate me in the Camden Cay motel. This was his *real* smile, a predator's show of teeth.

"You never showed up for your extraction," he continued. "I was worried you got flatlined. Until I started seeing your destructive fingerprints all over the mega. Attacking a TaoCom facility, Jack? What kind of people have you gotten wrapped up with?"

"Better people than you, dickhead," I growled. "You tried to kill me!"

Z rushed to my side, probably after hearing the change in conversational tone. "Goodwin, you piece of shit," he snapped. "Are your corpo masters demanding more tribute? You need to steal more of *my* work?"

Goodwin laughed. It was cold and as completely devoid of emotion as his smile.

"I've taken enough of your work, old friend," he said. "Now I'm just going to take everything else. Your little crew of misfits. Your smuggling operation. All those little underground rat nests you have hidden around the city.

"This is the endgame, Z. It came a little sooner than I would have wanted, but you forced my hand."

"And how did I do that, *Associate*?" Z asked.

"You got involved," Goodwin replied. "Playing your little rebel games at street level is one thing. But meddling in the affairs of giants..." Goodwin wagged his finger and clucked his tongue.

"I don't know what you're talking about," said Z.

"Look, Zoroaster, I need to talk to Jacqueline, and you're boring me."

Z's eyes narrowed as he watched the Overwatch Associate punch his finger at a desk terminal in front of him.

"Go take care of that, and let us talk," Goodwin continued with a casual wave of his hand.

A deep howl of pain erupted from the other side of the room. I leaped to my feet, and spun to face the noise.

Pilky was spasming out of control. The Brit thrashed in his NetOps chair, the howl turning into a gurgle. Z rushed over, and I moved to follow.

"Wait!" Goodwin shouted. "Let your friend handle it. We still need to talk."

My eyes darted between the smiling corpo snake and the center of the room where Z was fighting to shove a hypo-syringe into Pilky's neck.

"What do you want?" I shouted at the terminal. "Stop whatever you're doing to him, and I'll talk!"

"It's too late for him," Goodwin said. "I injected him with Zoraster's kill code. Did he tell you that he was the one who created it? No matter."

I looked back. Pilky wasn't moving, and Z was now yanking cables from various hardware stacks along the wall.

"One lowlife psycher zeroed," Goodwin said nonchalantly. "That's a slow day for me. But the list of people you can still save is very long, Jacqueline. So sit down."

I glared at the man on the monitor. My fists clenched so tightly that I could hear the graphene bones creaking in my left hand.

"Get fucked," I replied.

Goodwin laughed. The urge to put my fist through the screen was unbearable.

"Come on," he said through the trailing end of his chuckle. "Sit down." Then his smile disappeared for the first time. His eyes hardened in an instant shift of demeanor that sent chills of the sociopathic variety right through me.

"Come on, Jack," he growled. "Don't you want to know where Alice is?"

INTO THE LOOKING GLASS

Book Two of the *Jack:* Cyberpunk Series

Jack might have to cut a deal with this bastard, Goodwin. Not something she's all about, considering he already tried to kill her once. These things are never easy, are they?

But Alice needs Jack's help, and in saving her friend, Jack may get a chance to learn more about her secret implant and the power it holds.

What about Z and the crew? It's looking like the next big job will take them above the clouds into HighHold – right into the city of giants.